not even a tiny part of herself, just in case this never went beyond tonight.

It was a risk for a woman like her, giving everything to a man who'd sworn off marriage for good. She knew it, too. She'd taken almost the same vow, but hers had been tempered with *I will only marry again if I meet the perfect man.*

Well, no one was perfect, but Ry Hardin was darned close. She was already feeling emotionally committed to him, and if he didn't reciprocate, she could be in for some big-time heartache.

But what else was new? Wasn't she so used to heartache that she wouldn't know how to behave if it should suddenly disappear?

In the next heartbeat she wasn't thinking about anything....

Dear Reader,

THE BLACK WATCH returns! The men you found so intriguing are now joined by women who are also part of this secret organization created by BJ James. Look for them in *Whispers in the Dark,* this month's MAN OF THE MONTH.

Leanne Banks's delightful miniseries HOW TO CATCH A PRINCESS—all about three childhood friends who kiss a lot of frogs before they each meet their handsome prince—continues with *The You-Can't-Make-Me Bride.* And Elizabeth Bevarly's series THE FAMILY McCORMICK concludes with *Georgia Meets Her Groom.* Romance blooms as the McCormick family is finally reunited.

Peggy Moreland's tantalizing miniseries TROUBLE IN TEXAS begins this month with *Marry Me, Cowboy.* When the men of Temptation, Texas, decide they want wives, they find them the newfangled way—they *advertise!*

A Western from Jackie Merritt is always a treat, so I'm excited about this month's *Wind River Ranch*—it's ultrasensuous and totally compelling. And the month is completed with *Wedding Planner Tames Rancher!,* an engaging romp by Pamela Ingrahm. There's nothing better than curling up with a Silhouette Desire book, so enjoy!

Regards,

*Lucia Macro*

Senior Editor

---

Please address questions and book requests to:
Silhouette Reader Service
U.S.: 3010 Walden Ave., P.O. Box 1325, Buffalo, NY 14269
Canadian: P.O. Box 609, Fort Erie, Ont. L2A 5X3

# JACKIE
# MERRITT
# WIND RIVER RANCH

SILHOUETTE *Desire*

™ Published by Silhouette Books

America's Publisher of Contemporary Romance

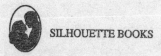

SILHOUETTE BOOKS

ISBN 0-373-76085-X

WIND RIVER RANCH

Copyright © 1997 by C.J. Books, Inc.

**Books by Jackie Merritt**

---

## JACKIE MERRITT

and her husband live just outside of Las Vegas, Nevada.
An accountant for many years, Jackie has happily traded
numbers for words. Next to family, books are her greatest joy. She started writing in 1987 and her efforts paid
off in 1988 with the publication of her first novel. When
she's not writing or enjoying a good book, Jackie dab-
bles in watercolor painting and likes playing the piano in
her spare time.

# Prologue

Carrying her medical bag, purse and an assortment of file folders, Dena Colby walked into her primary place of employment, Meditech Home Care, which consisted of an office in the front of the building and a lab in the back. It was nearly six, and she was through for the day except for returning the files she had used for today's appointments and checking her schedule for tomorrow's. She was currently working days, although all of the employees' shifts fluctuated on a twenty-four hour basis. Dena was an RN and enjoyed working for a company that supplied around-the-clock home nursing visits when prescribed by a physician.

There were only a few people in the office, one of whom was the receptionist, Gail Anderson. Gail was talking on the phone and she waved and motioned at Dena. "One moment, please. Dena just came in. I'm going to put you on hold while I transfer your call to her phone."

Dena deposited her load on her desk. "Who is it, Gail?" Wearily she sank into her chair. It had been a busy day, and she was tired, definitely ready to go home, have a hot shower and put up her feet.

"A man named Ryson Hardin. He said it was urgent that he speak to you as soon as possible. He's on line three, Dena."

Dena frowned slightly. "I don't know a Ryson Hardin. How urgent could a stranger's call be?" She stared at the blinking light of line three on her telephone for a few seconds, then rather belligerently reached for the receiver. If Hardin was using "urgent" to try to sell her something, she was apt to let him know what she thought of such tactics. She spoke coolly. "This is Dena Colby. What can I do for you?"

She heard the man clear his throat. "Miss Colby, this is Ry Hardin. I used your father's personal telephone directory to locate you. I...have some very bad news."

Dena gripped the telephone tighter as a barrage of emotions and memories struck mercilessly. "What sort of bad news?" she asked, the sharpness of her voice caused by a sudden acute fear.

"It's about your father. Simon...died this morning."

It didn't sink in. Dena sat there statue still, holding the phone to her ear without saying anything.

"Miss Colby, did you hear what I said?" Ry asked. He'd expected shock, but he hadn't anticipated total silence from Simon's daughter. He hadn't wanted to be the person to call Dena Colby, but the only other candidate for the discomfiting job was Nettie Bascomb, the housekeeper, and Nettie was up there in years and so shaken over Simon's death she was all but incoherent.

Dena's thoughts were beginning to coalesce. But denial was rampant in her system. This had to be some sort of cruel joke. "Who did you say you are?"

"Ryson Hardin. I've been the foreman on your father's Wind River Ranch for three years, Miss Colby. I'm surprised my name isn't familiar."

He doesn't know, Dena thought dully. Mr. Hardin did not know Colby family history. There were people who could have told him, Nettie for one. But maybe Nettie had left the ranch, for some reason, since their last correspondence.

"What happened?" Dena asked in a lifeless voice.

"To Simon?"

"Of course to Simon," she replied impatiently. "Who else would I be asking about?"

"Sorry," Ry said gently, realizing the shock he'd anticipated from Dena Colby was beginning to develop. "Dr. Worth thinks it was a cerebral hemorrhage. He can't say for sure without an autopsy, which, of course, is your decision to make. The doc believes it happened some time this morning. Your father had taken a pickup truck and gone to the south end of the ranch early this morning. No one—the ranch hands, Nettie and myself—was alarmed when he wasn't back by noon. Simon rarely announced or explained his plans for the day. By three I began wondering, however, and I asked Nettie if Simon had taken lunch with him. When she said no, I had everyone start looking for him."

Dena's voice had become quite hoarse. "And you found him dead." In the far recesses of Dena's mind was the fact that Nettie was still at the ranch. It was small comfort at this moment, but somewhat relieving regardless.

"Not me, personally, but yes." Two of the hands had spotted Simon's pickup from a hilltop. They were on horseback, and had ridden hard and fast from that hill to the truck. Simon was still in the driver's seat, slumped over the wheel. Dr. Worth's opinion was that he had died instantly. Ry didn't think he needed to explain every tiny detail to Dena Colby during this call, figuring that she had enough to digest with what he'd already told her.

He couldn't possibly grasp the true nature of Dena's state of mind. She could just barely think; her heart was pounding hard enough to hear and her hands were shaking like twigs in a high wind. Her mouth was so dry that speaking was almost impossible.

"I—I'll catch the first flight out," she mumbled thickly.

"If you let me know your flight schedule, I'll meet your plane, Miss Colby."

"I..." She was beginning to crack. Her father had died without forgiving her. He was too young to die, barely fifty years old, and now there was no longer a chance of forgiveness, of reconciliation. "Th-thank you for calling. I'll be in touch." She put down the phone.

"Dena?" It was Gail, looking at her across several desks with a worried expression. "Are you all right?"

"My...my father died this morning," Dena said in a choked whisper.

"Oh, Dena, I'm so sorry." The phone rang and Gail sent it an irritated look before answering it.

There was a self-protective numbness in Dena's system, which she knew had to be dispelled. She had to call the airlines for a flight from Seattle to Casper, Wyoming, and another from Casper to Lander...and rearrange her work schedule with Gail...and go home and pack. And all she wanted was to sit there and do nothing.

These days Dena didn't concern herself with the concept of *pretty*. She wore her nearly black hair short for the sake of convenience. Lipstick and blusher—used sparingly—were her only cosmetics. Her clothing was purchased with comfort in mind, and she didn't even own a cocktail dress, as she had rarely dated since her divorce three years ago, and those occasions had always been strictly casual. She lived a quiet life with one all-consuming goal, to reconcile with her father, who had stated angrily, sternly and emphatically that he would never speak to her again when she had rebelled against his insistence she go to college and instead had married Tommy Hogan right out of high school. At the time she hadn't cared how Simon felt about it. He'd been an overly strict parent with—in her opinion—unrealistic, old-fashioned ideas of how she should live her life.

It was only later on, when Tommy had proved to be the lazy, immature and not very honest person that Simon had declared him to be, that Dena realized in this case her father had been right. The whole Hogan family—dozens of them— were cut from the same cloth. Regardless of the many clashes with her father, Dena had absorbed Simon's ethics and standards. The Hogans, including Tommy, had had no ethics. It had been quite a blow for Dena to look at her husband one day, who'd been unshaven, out of a job again and hanging around their pathetic little house in town drinking one can of beer after another, and realize what a horrible mistake she had made. Tommy was not going to change and suddenly turn into the kind of man she had thought him to be before their marriage.

Or maybe she hadn't thought at all, beyond his handsome face and happy-go-lucky personality, she had decided with a sick feeling in her stomach.

That very day she had driven out to the ranch with the intention of making amends with her father. She had walked into the house, and Simon had immediately left it without a word. Nettie had smiled weakly. "Hello, honey. How are you?"

Dena's knees had given out, and she'd folded onto a chair. "He hasn't forgiven me, has he?" she'd said to the housekeeper. "Will he ever?"

Nettie had looked as though she didn't know where to put herself. Finally she had offered what she'd obviously thought was consolation. "Give him a little more time, honey."

Time had done nothing. In almost five years, while Dena had been getting her life on track, obtaining a divorce—which had infuriated the Hogan clan to the point of some of them telling terrible lies about her that had gotten back to Dena—leaving Winston, the small town where she had attended school and then lived after her marriage, moving to Seattle and entering a nursing program while holding down a job to support herself and her education, and finally receiving her nursing certificate and acquiring her present position with Meditech, she had tried contacting her father too many times to count. Her letters had not been returned, but neither had they been answered. Simon had never come to the phone when she'd called the ranch. True to his word, he had not spoken one syllable to her, either aloud or by mail.

And now he was gone.

Nausea roiled in Dena's stomach, and she also felt cold and sweaty. She knew the signs; if she didn't do something she was going to faint. Pushing her chair back from the desk, she leaned over and put her head between her knees. Vaguely she registered Gail saying goodbye to whomever she'd been talking with on the phone.

Then Gail was next to her, squatting to be on her level and rubbing Dena's back. "You're white as a sheet. I have some water. Can you take a drink?"

Slowly Dena sat up. "Yes, thanks." Accepting the paper cup of water, she sipped. "I felt as though I was going to black out."

Gail's expression was sympathetic. "I know."

"I'm okay now. I...I have to call the airlines."

"I'll do it for you. When do you want to leave?"

"Tonight, if possible." She and Gail were friendly enough for Gail to know that she was from Wyoming. But she hadn't told anyone about the heartrending break with her father, or the details of her unhappy and truly ludicrous marriage. Dena sometimes wondered why she had rebelled against her only living parent to the point of hurting herself, but it wasn't a subject that she could discuss with even her closest friends.

"Seattle to Casper, right?" Gail asked.

Dena nodded. "Then Casper to Lander."

"You just sit there and get yourself together. I'll call the airlines right now." With an air of efficiency—which was completely sincere as Gail Anderson was an extremely competent woman—the receptionist returned to her desk and began looking through the phone book.

Dena still felt numb, and maybe it was best, she reasoned. If her emotions started running wild, she might not have the strength to see this through.

And strength, both physical and emotional, was going to be crucial in the next few days. As dull-witted as her mind seemed to be at the present, she at least knew that much.

# One

Returning to Wyoming was traumatic for Dena. It was something she had wanted to do for so long, and to be going now under these conditions was almost incomprehensible. Anxiety ate at her during the flight from Seattle to Casper, and again on the much smaller plane bound for Lander. For some reason, she couldn't picture the ranch without her father. It wasn't that she didn't believe Ryson Hardin—no one would be so cruel as to call a woman with a lie of that nature—but envisioning the place without Simon was next to impossible.

At the same time, sitting stiffly in her seat, Dena wondered why she wasn't weeping. Her throat had felt tight and achy since Mr. Hardin's call, but she had not shed one tear. Unquestionably she suffered the sorrow one would expect to feel from such news, and yet she wasn't able to release the tight grip she had on her emotions. In truth, she felt as though she were trapped in some sort of terrible nightmare, and in the back of her mind was the childlike knowledge that nightmares lasted only a short while. It was such an inane sensation—she was an intelligent woman and fully cognizant of the difference between a nightmare and reality—and yet she couldn't eradicate it.

The plane landed at the Lander airport at three in the morning. She should have been exhausted and wasn't; obviously she was running on adrenaline.

Deplaning with the handful of other passengers arriving in Lander at this unholy hour, Dena walked through the gate and glanced around, ardently hoping to see Nettie. She had called the ranch, once she'd known her flight schedule, and Ry Hardin had answered almost immediately, as though he'd been sitting near the phone waiting for it to ring. Dena had been hoping to hear Nettie's voice, but when she'd asked about the older woman, Hardin had said she was in her room, ostensibly lying down.

"This has hit her pretty hard, Miss Colby," he'd said.

"Maybe...maybe she will feel up to meeting my plane," Dena had said unsteadily. But then she'd told Ry Hardin her arrival time, and he had said that he would be at the terminal.

Nevertheless, the hope that she would see Nettie instead of a stranger waiting for her was still with her. That hope faded away as she saw a man walking toward her. Without a dram of genuine interest in Hardin himself, she took in his physical appearance. He was a tall, rugged-looking man with dark hair and eyes. His clothing was jeans, boots and a hat that he removed and held in his right hand as he approached her. He looked as much like a rancher as any man she'd ever seen.

"Dena Colby?"

"Yes."

"I'm Ry Hardin. Do you have luggage?"

"One bag."

"We'll collect it and be on our way. You must be tired."

"No...no, I'm fine."

Ry looked at her curiously. She was an attractive woman, small and slender, dressed in navy slacks, a white blouse and a navy cardigan sweater, unbuttoned. She did not appear to be devastated, as he'd thought might be the case, although her eyes were a little too bright. Feverishly bright, he amended in his private assessment of Simon's daughter.

They walked to the baggage department, and Dena's one suitcase appeared almost at once. Ry carried it and escorted her outdoors to his vehicle. Rather, it was a ranch vehicle, Dena realized when she read the sign on the door: Wind River Ranch. It was then she remembered that all of the ranch's vehicles bore that same sign.

She also realized there were many details about her home that she hadn't thought of in years. Her concentration regarding anything in Wyoming had been focused almost entirely on her father. She bit down on her bottom lip painfully hard. She didn't want to do this. She didn't want to walk into the house she'd grown up in and feel its emptiness.

They were well under way before either said anything. Ry spoke first. "Nettie said you're a nurse."

Dena jumped and turned her gaze to the man behind the wheel. She had actually forgotten he was there. "Pardon?" she said.

Ry repeated himself and added, "Nursing is an admirable profession. One of my sisters in Texas is a nurse."

Dena tried to think of a response. She liked making new friends, and Ry Hardin seemed like a nice guy. But these were not ordinary circumstances, and there was no way she could concentrate on small talk.

She quietly murmured, "That's nice," and then unconsciously turned her face to the side window, again immersed in the agony of why she was in Wyoming in the middle of this dark night.

Her spiritless reply relayed her state of mind to Ry, who decided to say no more. If she instigated a conversation during the drive, he would, of course, participate. But he didn't expect that would occur, and he drove with his gaze straight ahead on the road.

After a few miles, however, he did say something else. He'd gone through the same shock and grief that Dena Colby was suffering right now with each of his own parents, and he wanted to let her know that he, too, was affected by Simon's sudden death. "I'm very sorry about your father, Miss Colby. I liked working for him. And I respected him."

Drawing a breath, Dena pulled herself out of the doldrums enough to answer. "Thank you. And call me Dena," she said. Colby was her legal name again, as she had petitioned the court for resumption of her maiden name at the time of her divorce, which had further infuriated the Hogans, who had already been incensed over the divorce. That was when she'd started hearing some of the completely groundless lies they had been spreading around town about her, and it was also when she'd made her decision to leave Wyoming. There'd been no chance of a career in any field in Winston, and she had wanted to make something of her life. She remembered now that she had also hoped that her leaving the area would shake her father's determination to disown her.

It hadn't worked.

As for Ry Hardin liking and respecting Simon, she didn't doubt it. If memory served her correctly, Simon had usually gotten along with his hired hands. In fact, he had gotten along with most people. It was only with her, his daughter, his only child, that he'd been so hard and unyielding.

Dena released a long sigh of utter anguish and stared through the window again. The countryside was familiar even in the dark, and she attempted to force herself to concentrate on landmarks. Anything was better than thinking of her reason for at long last coming home.

But thoughts of home and the past would not be squelched, and she finally stopped fighting them. Besides, not all of her memories were painful. Her mother, for instance, had been completely kind and loving. While Opal Colby had been alive, Dena had been a happy child.

And Simon had been a happier, more just man. Yes, now that she thought about it, he hadn't been so strict and demanding while his wife had lived.

And neither had Dena been so rebellious, she had to admit. In retrospect it seemed that once Opal's sweet and gentle ways were no longer a buffer in the family, there was no family. Simon went his way every day, detouring only long enough to make sure Dena was behaving herself, which meant no makeup, the right kind of reading material and television programs—only his opinion counted, of course—very little time on the phone and a dozen other symbolic slaps in the face.

At least that was the way Dena had interpreted her father's harshly issued orders and oft-repeated remarks of disapproval. For a girl in the throes of puberty who had so recently lost her mother, life was miserable. Many times she had muttered to herself that she hated her father, which had not been the truth at all. What she'd wanted so much she had ached from it was for him to hug her, speak kindly to her, tell her he loved her and even tuck her into bed at night as he had sometimes done before her mother's death.

Now, as an adult with medical training, Dena knew that when her mother died Simon hadn't been able to overcome his grief. He'd become hard because of internal misery, and as he hadn't understood the emotional ups and downs of a teenager, he had continued to treat Dena as the child she had once been. He could handle a child; he hadn't known how to deal with a budding woman. Dena had written of these things in her letters, but to her knowledge Simon had never read one of them. It was heartbreaking to envision him having destroyed or discarded her letters without opening them, but what else could she think?

The lights of Winston—still some miles ahead—gave her a jolt. She sat up a little straighter, wishing there was a way to reach the ranch without driving through the town. There were so many bad memories connected to Winston—her marriage, the Hogan family and their lies, her divorce, the fact that everyone in town knew her father would not say hello to her should they meet on the street. It was the way of small towns everywhere: everyone knew everyone else's business. She had not once missed Winston or anyone living there, and she felt no guilt over feeling that way, either.

Ry noticed her more alert attitude and thought it a good sign. With her having been raised on a ranch, Winston was the closest thing she had to a hometown. His own past was similar; he'd grown up on a ranch in Texas near a town that was about twice the size of Winston, and he had many fond memories of his school years in that town.

Ry slowed down to the speed limit as they passed the town limits. Not a car was moving on the main street, not a person was in sight. The windows of some buildings were lighted. Winston was beginning to wake up, but it was still so very early, just approaching dawn.

"You must have gone to school here," Ry said.

"Yes," Dena said, offering no further information.

Ry sighed inwardly, but he couldn't take offense at Dena Colby's reticence. She had to be hurting, and since she hadn't come home to visit her father during Ry's employment at the Wind River Ranch, he really couldn't begin to guess what was going on in her mind. Guilt, perhaps? He was suddenly curious about something he'd never even thought about before. *Why* hadn't Dena come home for three years? It might have even been longer than that, as his knowledge of Dena's absence was limited to his employment on the ranch.

In the next instant he realized that her dignity was very much like Simon's. Had he ever seen Simon Colby lose control of his temper, for example? Or let anyone into his inner thoughts? Yes, Ry thought, he had liked and respected his employer, but he had never felt close enough to the man to call him a friend.

The ranch lay twenty miles on the other side of Winston. Dena felt the rigidity of her body relax some when they were again on the open road, although she was still tenser than normal. She gulped hard. It wouldn't be long now, less than a half hour, and then the true nightmare would begin. She tried to think of something else. The question of how many times she had traveled the distance between the ranch and Winston came to mind. She knew every inch of this stretch of road, every curve and dip, except for—

"The road has been paved," she said in surprise, more to herself than to Ry.

But he heard and thought she was speaking to him. "Wasn't it paved when you lived here?"

"It was gravel."

"Probably been a lot of changes made in the area since you

moved to Seattle,'' Ry said. He wasn't trying to be snide or judgmental. His comment seemed perfectly normal to him.

Dena's head jerked around. "What do *you* know about my leaving?" She'd been under the impression that he knew nothing of Colby family history, but now she wondered. And if he did know of her and Simon's sad relationship, who had told him? Was she still the victim of lies and gossip around Winston? She didn't mind anyone knowing the truth of her past, but she despised the possibility of even a stranger believing some of those lies.

Ry was startled by the defensive tone of her voice and became a little defensive himself. "I don't know anything about you, so don't get your dander up at me. Your business is yours and mine is mine. That's the way I live my life."

She felt properly chastised and said no more on that subject. Truth was, which she was fully aware of, she was overly sensitive about the past. She should not have spoken to Ry Hardin in such an abrasive manner. Why wouldn't he snap back at her?

Besides, he'd been nice enough to crawl out of bed in the middle of the night to meet her plane, and she appreciated it.

"I haven't thanked you for picking me up," she said. "Let me do so now. I...I haven't been myself since your call."

"Forget it," Ry said quickly. "I know you've got a lot on your mind."

She put her head back and closed her eyes. "Yes, I do," she said in a near whisper. There was something warm and friendly about Ry Hardin, which she would have been happy to pursue at any other time. But she wasn't going to be in Wyoming long enough to concern herself with new friendships. She had arranged a week away from her job, figuring seven days should be a long enough time to deal with the morbid and heartbreaking details of burying her father. Her eyes squeezed more tightly shut for a moment. Could she get through the upcoming week without a breakdown? She felt on the verge of one, although she'd never experienced any such affliction before. But she'd worked with patients who had lost every hold on their senses because of a shock or even just the

rigors of ordinary, everyday life. The thought of mental in-
capacitation was horrifying; she *had* to maintain an even keel,
no matter how emotionally devastating the next few days
might prove to be.

Ry was surprised and pleased that Dena hadn't become angry over his defensive comeback. Even more pleasing was her
remembering to thank him right after what could have been a
serious breach between them. Obviously she was basically a
nice person, and he himself would much rather be friends than
enemies with anyone. Besides, it wasn't his intention to alien-
ate Simon's daughter. It had crossed his mind that Dena could
be his boss now. It was certain that someone was going to
have to take over Simon's duties, and why wouldn't that person be Simon's only child?

Not that Ry would ever kiss up to anyone to keep a job.
But he liked living and working at the six-thousand-acre Wind
River Ranch. He liked Wyoming, for that matter, and he
would rather stay on at the Colby ranch than start looking for
another job, no matter who picked up the reins.

Dena knew the mile-long ranch driveway was fast approaching, and her hands nervously clenched on her lap. Painful thoughts darted through her mind. She should have found
a way to force her father to talk to her. Why had it never
occurred to her that time might run out? The unhappiness that
was so much a part of her life was her fault. If she had returned
to the ranch before this, and followed Simon around until he
grew weary of the silence between them, she would not be
coming home now with such a heavy heart.

"Here we are," Ry murmured, making the turn onto the
ranch road. He sent his passenger a glance, and saw her sitting
stiffly still and staring out the front window. His heart reached
out to her. Losing a loved one was a hell of a thing to go
through. Whatever kind of woman Dena Colby was, she was
another human being, and he felt her grief in his own soul.

At first sight of the ranch house and outbuildings, illumi-
nated by yard lights on tall poles, Dena caught her breath and
held it. She felt light-headed from a lack of oxygen before she

finally breathed again, and by that time Ry had braked to a stop next to the house. He turned off the engine.

"I'll get your suitcase," he told her, implying that she should just get out, go inside and not concern herself with her luggage.

"Thank you." Her hand crept to the door handle. There were lights on in the house, and she suddenly knew that Nettie was waiting for her. Mobility returned in a rush, and she pushed open the door, got out and hurried to the back of the house. Taking the three steps to the porch, she crossed it quickly and opened the door that led to a mud room and then the kitchen.

Nettie materialized, her long, gray hair still in her nighttime braid, and wearing a robe and slippers. With tears running down her cheeks, she opened her arms.

"Child" was all she said.

Dena stepped into the circle of the older woman's arms, and that was when the dam broke. All of the tears she hadn't shed seemingly came at once. The two women held each other and sobbed together.

Ry passed them with Dena's suitcase and they never noticed. Feeling the sting of tears himself, he brought the suitcase to the bedroom that Nettie had told him had always been Dena's.

Then he let himself out the side door of the house and walked down to the barn. He always got up early; today was just a few hours earlier than usual. Grabbing a shovel, he began cleaning stalls.

Although this was not one of his regular jobs on the ranch, it beat standing around and feeling bad by a mile.

# Two

At 8:00 a.m. Dena was on her way back to Winston. Using one of the ranch cars, she drove the familiar road, thankful that it was sparsely traveled, as her mind was too overloaded to concentrate on anything but the sudden tragic turn of her life.

She felt rocky from lack of sleep and because she hadn't been able to eat more than a few bites of toast this morning. She knew what she was doing to herself. Even people without medical training knew that one shouldn't stop sleeping and eating because of a shock. But that's what people with a heart did, wasn't it? The kind of shock she had received, the nightmare she was living through, all but disabled a person. Certainly it destroyed normal routines and habits, and only God knew how and when she was going to regain her usual sensibilities.

Dena harbored an impossible wish: that she could avoid Winston altogether. But it was where Dr. Worth's office was located, and Nettie had told Dena that the doctor had to see her posthaste. Dena was certain she knew why—that question of an autopsy.

The funeral home was also in Winston. If Dena had the power to eliminate one day from her life, this would be it. There were others that had caused an enormous amount of trouble and grief, but none to compare with what today demanded of her.

Dr. Worth had been the Colby family physician for as long as Dena could remember, and Nettie had said that his office was still in the same place it had always been. Once Dena reached the town limits, it took only a few minutes to get there. There was a small parking strip next to the building, and she pulled into a space and turned off the ignition. Panic rose in her throat. She didn't want to do this. Neither did she want to visit the funeral home after talking to Dr. Worth and plan her father's burial. How did one converse coherently and with a reasonable amount of intelligence about such things?

Tears welled and she wiped them away with a tissue. Then, drawing a deep breath, she took her purse and got out of the car. She had phoned Dr. Worth at his home this morning and he had told her to meet him at his office at eight-thirty. She was right on time.

With every cell in her body throbbing like a toothache, she walked to the side door of the building—another of Dr. Worth's instructions—and rang the bell. The door opened almost at once. Dr. Worth gave her a quiet smile. "Hello, Dena. Come in."

"Hello, Doctor," she whispered hoarsely.

He led her to his personal office and sat her in a chair near his desk. Even through the haze of pain clouding her mind, Dena realized that Dr. Worth had aged since she'd last seen him. She was thinking about the changes time wrought on everyone and everything when Dr. Worth spoke.

"I understand you're a nurse now," he said, seating himself at his desk.

"Yes."

"Then you'll have a better understanding of what we must discuss."

"You want to do an autopsy."

"No, I have to know if *you* want an autopsy."

Dena swallowed the lump in her throat. "The ranch foreman said you diagnosed the cause of Dad's death as a cerebral hemorrhage."

"I did, and I still believe my initial diagnosis. But if you have any doubts…"

"Was there any chance of foul play?"

"Oh, no, nothing like that. Simon died quite naturally. It's just that sometimes family members are driven to know the exact and precise cause of death."

"I don't feel that way, Doctor. Unless there is good reason for an autopsy, I don't want it."

Dr. Worth nodded approvingly. "I'm glad to hear that. Dena, you have to know how sorry I am about Simon's death. How are you holding up?"

Dena turned her face away. "Not…well," she said in an unsteady voice.

"You look drawn and exhausted, but that's to be expected, I suppose, when you flew all night to get here. Are you eating?"

"Not…much," she whispered.

Dr. Worth eyed her thoughtfully. "One of life's most traumatic experiences is the death of a loved one. There's a hole in the world that wasn't there before, an emptiness within oneself, and the memories we carry of that person seem to bombard us with cruel clarity. We tend to feel guilty over every disagreement with that person and any event where we think we might have done things differently."

"I *could* have done things differently, Doctor."

"But the problems you and Simon had are long in the past, Dena," Dr. Worth said gently. "You must try not to dwell on what happened so many years ago."

Dena's eyes dropped to her hands on her lap. She could tell the good doctor that nothing had changed during those years, that she had tried and tried to reconcile with her father and he had died without forgiving her. She could talk for an hour about the letters she'd written and the phone calls she'd made, but what good would it do?

All she said was, "I'll try, Doctor."

"Good," he replied, appearing satisfied that his little pep talk had worked.

Dena rose from her chair. "I won't take up any more of your time, Dr. Worth. Thank you for seeing me." She started for the door, then something occurred to her and she stopped and turned. "Was Dad getting regular checkups, Doctor?"

"Simon rarely showed his face in this office, Dena. Essentially he was a very healthy man."

"Then he wasn't on any medication that you know of?" There were some drugs that could wreak havoc with the circulatory system, and if Simon was taking *any* kind of medication, she wanted to know what it was.

"If he was, he didn't get it from me. Dena, try to take comfort from the swiftness of Simon's death. He died too young, but the way he went was much better than a long, lingering illness."

Dena hated remarks like that, even though she knew Dr. Worth was still attempting to ease her pain and there was even some truth in what he'd said.

But suddenly she couldn't talk about her father's death a second longer. "Thank you for your time, Doctor," she repeated and hurried out.

In her car it occurred to her then that she might run into someone she knew while in Winston, a thought that nearly brought on a fit of hysteria. Holding her hand to her throat, she took several deep breaths and told herself to calm down. She might as well face the fact that there wasn't a snowball's chance in hell of avoiding people's sympathy during her week in the area.

Or could she? Where was it written that she had to have a public service for her father? She could confine the sad event to— Groaning, she put her head in her hands. Nettie would be appalled. Dena could see herself and Nettie standing alone in the cemetery, listening to a prayer administered by...who? A minister? Someone from the funeral home? Oh, what a pitiful picture, she thought with a fresh gush of tears. And it would be an improper, insulting rite for a man of Simon Colby's stature. She was being selfish again, thinking of herself and the discomfort of a public display of grief.

Wiping her eyes, she put on dark glasses and forced herself to start the car. She would go to the funeral home and then get out of Winston. And if she ran into a dozen acquaintances—unlikely but possible—with vulturelike words of sympathy and only partially concealed expressions of morbid curiosity, she would handle it.

She had no choice.

That night Dena was able to eat dinner and to talk to Nettie without choking on her own words, probably because she felt so head-to-foot numb. It was even possible to walk through the house, remember her father and not fall apart. When she went to bed she was able to sleep, and any troubling dreams she had during those hours vanished when she awoke.

Ry thought she seemed unnaturally calm, not at all like the tense, jumpy, crushed woman he had picked up at the airport.

In truth, he didn't see all that much of her, as he took his meals with the men and slept in the bunkhouse. But once he spotted her walking outside, and when a load of barbed wire and posts were delivered the afternoon just before the day of the funeral, he took the invoice from the driver of the truck and went into the house. Nettie was in the kitchen with flour up to her elbows, kneading a large batch of bread dough. Nettie had always taken pride in the good meals she served Simon and his men, and her pragmatic attitude was that people had to eat whether she was grieving or not. She looked up as Ry walked in.

"I need to talk to Dena, Nettie." Nettie was a little bit of a woman, spry as a spring robin and much stronger than she looked. Ry estimated her age around sixty, but she could be ten years older or younger. Age, either his or hers, was not something they had discussed.

"I think she's in the living room," Nettie told him.

"Thanks." Ry left and headed for the living room. From

the doorway he saw Dena seated in a chair and staring blankly into space. Her vacant expression bothered him, and he wondered what, exactly, was going through her mind to cause it. Of course it had everything to do with Simon's death, he knew that, but weren't tears and sobs better than such concentrated stillness? Was she deliberately holding her emotions in check? That didn't seem very healthy to Ry.

But who was he to judge Dena's method of dealing with grief? Everyone on the ranch was affected by Simon's death, in one way or another. The men were unnaturally subdued, working without the wisecracks and tomfoolery they often engaged in. Nettie was carrying on in spite of her sorrow, and he had willingly taken over the operation of the ranch for the time being. Taken Simon's place, actually, although he felt certain that Dena would resent that concept should anyone voice it.

Well, he sure as hell wasn't going to say any such thing to Dena, but he did have to interrupt her present reverie. The invoice in his hand demanded a decision he didn't feel he should make.

"Dena?" he said.

Slowly her head came around. Her look of total disinterest struck him as one containing a question—who is this man walking into my father's living room? In truth she'd been miles into the past, thinking of her mother and envisioning how much differently things would have turned out had Opal lived.

She blinked, as though coming awake, and said, "Yes?"

Ry entered the room and walked over to her. "Dena, do you have the authority to sign checks for the ranch?"

She blinked again. "Whatever gave you that idea?"

Ry frowned. She seemed a million miles away and was speaking very slowly. Actually she seemed so withdrawn from reality that he started worrying about her. For certain he didn't like bothering her with business at a time like this, but he had no choice.

"I have an invoice here that's marked C.O.D.," he said,

"and someone has to write a check for $1,254.33. My name's not on the checking account. I was wondering if yours is."

Lines appeared in Dena's forehead. Why ever would he think such a thing? "Of course it's not," she said, becoming slightly more alert. She paused to think about the amount of the check he needed and ended up speaking a bit suspiciously. "What did you buy for twelve hundred dollars?"

That hint of suspicion in her voice didn't sit right with Ry. Grief stricken or not, Dena had no right to intimate that he was anything but a hundred percent honest, which he was. His face hardened and so did his voice. "*I* didn't buy anything. Simon ordered barbed wire and posts to cross-fence one of the big pastures. The material has just been delivered, and the driver is waiting for payment."

His defensive tone startled Dena. Good Lord, couldn't she say anything to him without having her head bitten off? He'd done the same thing during the drive from the airport. What had she said then to cause such a reaction? Her head was aching and she couldn't remember the incident clearly.

But it didn't matter. She couldn't have mustered any genuine anger today if her life depended on it, especially not over something like this. "Ry, you're the foreman. You handle it, please."

"How?"

"I really don't care," she said listlessly.

Ry could hardly believe his ears. "You don't care. Dena, do you have any idea how many decisions have to be made nearly every day about something on this ranch? Do you care about that? Let me go one step further. Do you care about the ranch at all?"

Did she? It wasn't a question Dena had spent any time pondering. She'd grown up on this ranch, but did it mean anything to her? *Should* it mean something to her?

She didn't like that Ry Hardin had just brought to light a brand-new aspect of this ordeal.

"Just so you know," he said flatly, "this isn't the only situation where someone's going to have to write checks. I think you should do something about that."

"Like what?" She was truly puzzled by his attitude.

"Get your name on the checking account."

"And how do I accomplish that? Simply walk into the bank and tell someone I want access to my father's money?" Dena shook her head. "They'd either laugh me out of the bank or call the sheriff."

Ry looked at her for a long moment. "Call Simon's lawyer."

"I didn't know he had one."

"Well, he did. His name is John Chandler." Remembering the hell she was living through, Ry spoke with less tension. "Dena, hasn't it occurred to you that Simon probably left the ranch to you?"

It took a second for that unlikely idea to sink in, and when it finally did she retorted, "Don't make me laugh."

Ry felt thunderstruck. "Well, who else would he leave it to?"

"I haven't the foggiest." Dena waved her hand. She'd had enough of this conversation. In fact, she wanted to sink back into the hole Ry's appearance had pulled her out of. "Please go away. I don't want to talk about any of this."

"What you should be saying is that you don't want to *face* any of this." Ry shook his head. "I think you're in for one very big surprise, lady." Turning on his heel, he walked out.

"Oh, just shut up," Dena muttered wearily, but Ry was already gone and didn't hear her. It was just as well, she thought, although she was not going to put up with Ry Hardin or anyone else badgering her about the ranch. She was here for one week, and several days of that week were already over. The funeral was set for tomorrow. Someone had put an obituary in the newspaper announcing the time and place, so there would undoubtedly be a horde of people there.

But it would be her final agony. After tomorrow she could start returning to normal.

Dena laid her head back and looked at the ceiling. What *was* going to happen to the ranch? Did Ry really care or was he just concerned about his job?

She clenched her hands into fists. Damn him for giving her another worry, another reason to weep and feel helpless.

Outside, Ry walked back to the trucker. "There's no one to sign a check, so I can't pay you today. I could call your company and arrange a later payment, or you could take the wire and posts back to Lander."

The man shrugged. "Makes no difference to me. What d'ya wanna do?"

Ry thought for a moment. Why was he so shook about this? About Dena's disinterested attitude? To hell with it. If she didn't care what happened to her father's ranch, why should he? He probably wouldn't be here to put in that new fence, anyway.

"Take 'em back," he said, and gave the man the invoice. "If and when things ever get straightened out around here, we'll order again."

The man got into his truck and drove away.

There were two rooms in the house that Dena had been deliberately ignoring, her father's bedroom and his office. The mere thought of entering Simon's bedroom gave her cold chills. It was Nettie who had gone in and chosen the clothing for Simon's burial, and it was Ry who had delivered them to Andrews Funeral Home. Dena appreciated their consideration. Nettie's, she understood. Ry was a different matter. Ry bothered Dena in a strange way, one she couldn't quite put her finger on. When she thought of him, that is, which wasn't often. In fact, she was discovering that she was able to blank out her mind on many subjects. Maybe that was what overwhelming grief did to a person, she thought. If something was too painful to think about, you simply bury it so deep in your psyche it stayed buried.

Still, Ry's comments about the checking account and having to pay bills and such had penetrated the soothing fog Dena preferred over saber-sharp reality at the present, and she geared herself up for a look at ranch records. It was not something her father had ever invited her to do, but she had to concede the fact of her age before she'd left the ranch, and also the dissension that had existed between her and Simon.

A shiver rippled up her spine as she opened the office door and stepped in. The room was as drab as she remembered. Dull, dark paneling on the walls. Worn carpet. It was depressing. Old furniture, a musty odor. For that matter, the entire house was drab. Because of Nettie it was clean, but Dena was positive no one had done any interior painting or even changed the placement of one piece of furniture since she'd left the ranch at eighteen years of age.

To be painfully accurate, nothing had been changed or improved since her mother's death. Opal had been a natural-born homemaker, and everything in this old house that was now dull, nicked, snagged and all but ready for the junk pile had been bright and pretty and warmly inviting while she lived.

When Opal became ill, Simon had hired Nettie to take over the housekeeping and the preparation of meals for the ranch hands. Nettie had fit in at once. She and Opal had become close friends, and Nettie had suffered as much as Dena and Simon over Opal's courageous battle with cancer.

And then it was over and nothing had ever been the same. Dena swallowed hard. She could fall apart so easily, and she would if she let herself dwell on the past. The present was difficult enough to deal with; dredging up her mother's long illness and death was inviting disaster.

She shut the door behind her and walked over to the ancient desk Simon had used. There was a stack of ranching journals on one corner, a cup containing an assortment of pens and pencils about dead center, and some papers and file folders on the opposite corner. Dena sat in the old leather chair behind the desk and started to cry.

"Damn," she whispered. She hadn't come in here to cry. How was the human body able to produce as many tears as she had shed since her arrival home and Nettie's emotional welcome? She carried a pocketful of tissues, because even while blocking out what she could of the emotional trauma caused by her father's untimely death, tears would suddenly overwhelm her.

Taking one out, she wiped her eyes and blew her nose. Then she drew a deep breath and began opening drawers. In the bottom right-hand drawer she found a checkbook. Lifting it to the desk, she opened it. Seeing Simon's handwriting caused more tears, and this time she let them flow. If only she'd seen this wonderful scrawl in replies to the dozens of letters she had written him over the years. How could he have been so hard as to protect and maintain a vow of silence where his only child was concerned, especially when she had tried so hard to atone for her rebellious behavior? Surely he had heard about her and Tommy's divorce, and her departure from Winston.

But maybe he had also heard the lies that the Hogan clan had viciously spread far and wide about her.

Sighing helplessly, Dena again pulled out a tissue. Her still-damp eyes widened in surprise when she read the amount of money in this checking account—over sixty thousand dollars. Well, there was certainly enough money to pay any bills that might come up, and to handle the men's payroll for an extended period.

But it was in the bank and no one could sign checks. Maybe she had better call that lawyer, as Ry had suggested in a rather overbearing manner. Her hackles rose for a few moments. How dare Ry Hardin treat her as some kind of idiot child? Just who did he think he was?

Mumbling to herself about Ry being no more than an employee and acting like lord of the manor, Dena looked for and found her father's personal telephone directory. She flipped pages until she saw John Chandler's name and number, then reached for the phone and placed a call. After two rings a male voice came on the line.

"Hello. This is John Chandler. As I notified all my current clients of my vacation before I closed shop for two weeks, you must be unaware of my schedule. I will be back in the office on the fifteenth, so please either leave a message at the beep so I may return your call at that time, or call me again. Thanks for your patience."

The message startled Dena so much that she hung up rather

than identifying herself for John Chandler's recorder. The man was on vacation and obviously not aware of Simon's death. The fifteenth, Dena mused, glancing at the calendar on the wall. Four days away. Maybe she would still be here, maybe not.

But did she dare leave without solving the checkbook dilemma? *Someone* had to be given access to ranch money. The men couldn't work without pay, nor could the ranch function without supplies.

She sat back in her father's chair, stunned by the responsibility suddenly thrust upon her. She should not have to deal with this on top of her father's death.

But the problem was not going to vanish just because she wished it would.

What on earth was she going to do?

Frowning, she wondered if anyone knew where John Chandler had gone for his vacation. Was it possible that he'd gone nowhere and was merely resting at home?

No, if he was in the area he would have heard about Simon.

Wait a minute. If Ry knew Simon's lawyer was a man named Chandler, maybe he knew more—like, for instance, where he'd gone for his vacation. If she discovered the attorney's location, she wouldn't hesitate a moment in calling him. She needed legal advice, and the sooner the better.

Before going outside to look for Hardin, Dena went to her bathroom and washed her teary face. There was nothing to do about her puffy eyes except hold a cold, wet washcloth on them for a few minutes. It helped some, but there really was no way to conceal the ravages of so much sorrow. She brushed her hair and applied lipstick. It was the best she could do, and she left it at that.

Then she headed for the kitchen. Nettie was sniffling while she cut up chickens, breaking Dena's heart all over again. Battling her own raw and wounded emotions, she cleared her throat.

"Nettie, would you have any idea of where I might find Ry?"

"He was looking for you about a half hour ago."

"He found me and left. This is about something else."

"Oh. Well, I never have tried to keep track of the men, honey. He could be anywhere on the ranch."

"All right, thanks."

Leaving the house through the back door, Dena stopped to look around. To her surprise, she spotted Ry walking into the barn. It looked as if he was carrying a large coil of rope.

Hurrying across the expanse of ground between house and outbuildings, she entered the barn and called, "Mr. Hardin?"

In the tack room Ry heard her and disgustedly shook his head. So he was Mr. Hardin now. What a peculiar woman.

"In here," he yelled out. He pushed the coil of rope farther back on the shelf, fitting it in between other coils and some gallon containers of harness and leather oil. There were still harnesses hanging on wall hooks from the days when everything done on the ranch was accomplished with teams of horses. And saddles on racks, and bins of old horseshoes and metal parts and leather strapping to repair harnesses. As the tack room occupied a corner of the barn, there were two windows, one in each outside wall. Dust motes danced in the sun's rays coming in through the east window. Simon obviously had never thrown anything away, and from the day Ry started working on the Wind River Ranch he had itched to clean out this room. At least half of its contents should be hauled to the dump. Some of it, of course, was saleable. But in Ry's opinion, whatever was not needed in today's operation should be either sold or discarded.

Dena walked in. Rather, she stepped just inside the doorway and stopped. In the years since she'd left, not one single thing had changed in this room. It was the same as the house, she realized, in need of a thorough going over.

Her gaze moved to Ry, and she suddenly felt accusatory. He was the foreman and certainly could have fit a little tack room cleaning into his work routine. Even if he hadn't had the ambition to do it himself, he could have assigned the job to one or more of the other men.

"This place could use a good cleaning," she said flatly.

Ry was in no **mood** for snide remarks. Rather than agree

with her, which he most certainly did, he drawled, "Seems fine to me."

"Are you saying you don't see anything that could use some improvement in here?"

Because she sounded sarcastic, Ry took his time in looking around. When he finally brought his gaze back to her, he said, "I'm surprised you care about clutter and dust in here when you don't give a damn about the overall operation of the ranch. Must be the female in you."

Dena's face colored, but she shot back, "A sexist remark if I've ever heard one." Her mind, she realized, was shockingly dull, and for a few moments she couldn't remember why she was even in the tack room. Why on earth was she standing here and trading insults with this man?

Then it came to her. "The tack room is more your business than mine. Clean it or wallow in the dirt, it's all the same to me. The only reason I came out here was to find out if you knew where John Chandler went on his vacation."

"Didn't know he took one. I've only talked to him a couple of times. He's not my lawyer."

A dead end. Dena frowned and turned to leave.

"Hey," Ry called. "If you really want to run him down, you might try calling his secretary. Her name is Sheila Parks. It's possible she left town, too, but who knows?"

Dena stopped, one eyebrow raised. "Meaning she took her vacation the same time as her boss?"

Ry shrugged. "Makes sense to me."

It did make sense. "I would imagine Ms. Parks is listed in the telephone book."

"Beats me," Ry said. "And it's Mrs. Parks, but I don't know her husband's first name. Can't be that many Parks in the area, though."

"Thank you."

"You're welcome." Ry didn't like the way they'd talked to each other about the tack room. There was no earthly reason for them to bicker, and he decided then and there to turn things around. "Dena, I agree with you about cleaning up this place,'' he said quietly. "I've wanted to do it since I started working here.''

Relief flooded Dena's system over the drastic change in Ry's voice and demeanor. The last thing she wanted was to be at odds with anyone right now. "But Dad wouldn't let you, would he?''

Her perception surprised him, but why should it? If anyone had ever really known Simon Colby, it would be his daughter.

Ry took a step closer to her. "There's something else I'd like to say. I'm not normally short-tempered, and I've snapped at you more than once. I'm sorry for it and it won't happen again.''

She looked into his dark eyes and felt the sting of tears in her own. Her voice was husky when she spoke. "There's really no reason for you and me to disagree about anything. I'm sorry I was so sharp-tongued about the condition of this room. If I'd thought at all before sniping at you about it, it never would have happened.''

Ry nodded in understanding. "You're going through a bad time, and I guess you're entitled to a little sniping.''

"I'm not sure that even grief entitles a person to treat other people rudely.'' She managed a brave little smile that nearly broke Ry's heart. He had to forcibly stop himself from moving closer to her and pulling her into his arms. Strictly to comfort her, of course.

"See you later,'' she said then, and turned and left.

Ry walked to a window and watched her leave the barn and head for the house. Dena Colby aroused a complexity of emotions within him. Was it all because of the tragedy she was having to face more or less by herself, or was there more to it?

He wished he knew the answer to that question, because it suddenly seemed very important.

# Three

———

There were three Parks listings in the telephone book, two with a rural address, one in Winston. Dena tried the town number first. A female voice sang out a cheery, "Hello?"

"Hello," Dena said. "I'm trying to locate Sheila Parks, secretary to John Chandler. Is there any chance I might have reached her home?"

"Sheila's my mother-in-law, so you didn't miss it by much. Actually all three Parks in the directory are related. But that's beside the point, isn't it? Getting back to Sheila, she's not in the area right now. I'd be happy to take your number and have her call you when she returns."

Disappointed, Dena pressed on. "Would it be possible for you to tell me where she is, and if she can be reached by telephone?"

The woman was still friendly, but Dena noticed that a bit of reserve had entered her voice when she said, "Sheila's on vacation. Who did you say you are?"

"I'm sorry, but I didn't say. My name is Dena Colby, and it's really Mr. Chandler I need to speak to. I called his office and apparently he, too, is on vacation. Do you know where he went, by any chance? I wouldn't be bothering anyone about this if it wasn't extremely important. You see, Mr. Chandler is…was my father's attorney, and Dad…passed away quite…suddenly.'' It was so difficult to say, and Dena hadn't thought of that in advance. She cleared her throat and continued. ''I really need to talk to Mr. Chandler about…well, several things.''

''Please accept my condolences, Ms. Colby. I believe Sheila mentioned John and his wife vacationing in England. As far as reaching Sheila, she and Doug, my father-in-law, are traveling in their motor home. They could be almost anywhere, although they did talk about exploring the New England states. I'm sorry I can't be more help, but that's really all I know. Oh, except that they'll be back soon. Shall I ask Sheila to call you when she gets home?''

Dena thought a moment. ''No, that won't be necessary. Mr. Chandler will be back on the fifteenth, and I'll wait and talk to him. Thank you for speaking to me.''

''You're quite welcome. You said your last name is Colby. I just remembered reading Simon Colby's obituary. Is he your father?''

''Yes. Goodbye, Mrs. Parks.'' Dena put the phone down before Mrs. Parks could get in any more questions. Dena appreciated the woman's friendliness and trust, but the conversation had started getting uncomfortably personal.

She sighed heavily. Merciful God, how was she going to cope with it all?

But it wasn't a matter of merely coping as far as the ranch went, was it? No one could pay bills or write payroll checks. That was much more than an emotional upheaval. And what about supplies? Groceries?

Too worried to sit still, Dena left the office to find Nettie. The housekeeper was still in the kitchen.

''Nettie,'' Dena said, walking in. ''I'm afraid we have a real problem. How are you fixed for groceries?''

Nettie looked at her with some surprise. ''Land sakes, honey, you had me alarmed for a second. The cupboards, freezer and pantry are loaded with groceries. Why would you think that's a problem?''

"Because no one on the place can sign checks."

"Oh. Well, everyone will still have plenty to eat. You see, when I run short of supplies I drive to town and shop at Whitman's Food Mart. Simon arranged a charge account with Whitman's, so I wouldn't have to bother him about kitchen money. Land sakes, it's been that way for years and years. Don't you remember?''

"No, I don't remember." She still didn't. It hurt to think how self-centered she'd been in her teens, but facts were facts. Small wonder she and Simon had butted heads so often.

Dena rubbed the back of her neck. "Is there anything you'd like me to do, Nettie?''

"You mean help with the cooking?''

"Or anything else."

"No, honey. Don't concern yourself with the household chores. You have enough on your mind."

"I also have a splitting headache. I think I'll lie down for an hour or so."

"You go right ahead and do that."

Dena went to her bathroom, swallowed two over-the-counter headache pills with a drink of water, then continued on to her bedroom. Lying on her bed, she closed her eyes and slept.

The next morning Dena didn't even wonder if she would get through the funeral without falling apart. That soothing numbness had returned in the night, and she showered, dressed and ate a light breakfast on automatic pilot.

As she'd suspected, hordes of people attended the service. She had told the funeral director to make it as short and emotionless as possible. No singing, she'd said adamantly. No sad songs or eulogies. Simon Colby would not have wanted an emotion-filled service, with people weeping their hearts out because of soul-wrenching music, and neither did she.

To her chagrin, most of the attendees reconvened at the ranch to eat and talk about Simon. Everyone that came brought something, a cake, a casserole, a ham. It all passed in a blur for Dena, except for a few stand-out incidents. For one, she could hardly believe her eyes when Tommy was suddenly standing before her.

"Hello, Dena. Sorry about your dad, even if the old guy did give you and me a hard time."

She stared at the man to whom she'd once been married. Tommy was as handsome as ever, reeked of cologne and looked prosperous. But she would bet anything that he had either borrowed the money for the new clothes he was wearing, or he'd charged them. In her experience, Tommy had never set a dollar aside for an emergency, and she couldn't believe that irresponsible trait had evolved into thriftiness during her absence. What if she hadn't had a savings account when the call came about Simon's death? How would she have paid for her flight home?

"Hello, Tommy," she said, while marveling that she had once believed herself to be madly in love with this man. Of course, in those days she hadn't known that a handsome face was Tommy's one and only asset. In fact, looking at him now, she felt pity. It was an impersonal pity and in no way touched her soul. But it was sad that he had no ambition to better himself. She would be surprised if he even had a steady job.

He grinned at her, that cute grin that used to give her goose bumps. "You're looking good."

She smirked because she couldn't look worse if she'd tried. Oh, her black dress was attractive and her hair was nicely arranged, but her face was puffy and the tastefully small amount of makeup she had put on this morning was long gone.

"I'm surprised to see you here," she said. Recalling his initial remark about Simon giving them a hard time, she added, "Especially in light of your dislike of Dad."

"Hey, you didn't like him very much, either. And you had good reason. We both did. If he would have shelled out a few bucks when we needed it, we might still be married."

"It was not his place to 'shell out a few bucks,' Tommy. And if you care to remember, we *always* needed money. What did you expect him to do, give us a weekly paycheck? If you have the gall to blame Dad for the breakup of our marriage, don't tell me about it. Now, if you'll excuse me..."

She wound her way through the crowd, stopping briefly to accept condolences and words of sympathy, some of which she appreciated as they were from old friends of her father's, neighboring ranchers, for instance. Eventually she reached the other side of the room. She was glad to see Tommy leaving through the front door, and wondered why he had bothered to get all dressed up and attend the funeral of a man he'd despised. Surely he hadn't supposed she would be thrilled to see him. And how dare he make derogatory remarks about Simon, today of all days?

Had Tommy married her because he'd thought her father would support him? What a ghastly idea that was, but it probably should have occurred to her before this.

Still, it was water under the bridge and totally immaterial to not only today's events but to her life in general. She really had no feelings at all for Tommy. There were memories, of course, some good, some bad, but feelings? No, there were none within her.

Another incident that stood out occurred when most of the crowd had dispersed and only a few people remained in the living room. They were talking to Nettie. Dena hadn't eaten anything since breakfast, and she went to the kitchen. Nibbling on a piece of ham, she stared out the window over the sink with her back to the room.

She felt drained and empty. For years she had been passionate about reconciling with her father. Without that driving force gnawing at her vitals, life seemed rather purposeless. Could she simply go back to Seattle, her job and friends, and act as though she hadn't received the worst possible blow fate could have dealt her?

"Dena?" She turned slightly. Ry was standing there. "Are you all right?" he asked.

For the first time since she had met this man, she really saw him. He looked clean and crisp in his dark gray Western pants and shirt. There was a black string tie at his collar, and his black leather boots looked smooth as satin and shiny as a mirror. He wasn't as handsome as Tommy. Rather, his features weren't as perfectly arranged as Tommy's. But he was tall and strongly built, and there was a mature, outdoorsy handsomeness to his face that Tommy would never attain. Tommy relied on being cute and thought the world owed him a living; Ry earned his own way and would probably be insulted if anyone referred to him as cute.

"I'm okay," she told him. Ry had spoken to her before this today, but she honestly couldn't remember what he'd said. In fact, much that had occurred—at the cemetery, especially— had seemed to vanish from her mind. Temporary memory loss, she thought. A measure of self-protection. It was natural and normal, and she was glad she didn't recall every painful detail of the day.

Ry walked over to the table and took a cookie from a container. There was a lot of food left, and some plates and bowls to be returned to their owners when Nettie got her kitchen organized again.

Munching on the cookie, Ry looked at her. "I wanted to commend you for planning a sensible service."

"A funeral is bad enough without wringing every drop of emotion out of everyone attending it," she said quietly.

"Agreed. I arranged similar services for my parents."

"You've lost your parents, too? Do you have any other family?"

Ry recalled mentioning one of his sisters the night he'd picked her up at the airport, but saw no good reason to remind Dena of it. "Two sisters," he said. "They both live in Texas. I guess you're an only child."

"Yes." Dena was suddenly choked up. "I'd rather not talk about it."

Ry nodded. "Then we won't. Dena, about the ranch…"

She cut in. "I'd rather not talk about that, either, if you don't mind."

"All I was going to say was that you can count on me to be here for as long as you might need my help. It's pretty apparent that you don't know what's coming next, and while I feel Simon left you the ranch, I guess anything is possible.

Whatever happens, I'll hang around until you know your next move.''

"The other men won't."

"Why do you think that?"

"Can they work without paychecks? I don't think so."

"You just might be surprised about that. Besides, someone will have the authority to keep the ranch going, either you or a court-appointed manager."

Dena frowned. "Are you saying that if Dad didn't leave the ranch to me, the court will take over?"

"The state, Dena, and only if there's no will. As methodical a man as Simon was, I can't believe he didn't have a will. Have you talked to John Chandler yet?"

"He's out of town until the fifteenth."

"Well, that's only a few days away."

"But I might not be here."

Ry looked startled. "You're not thinking of leaving so soon, are you?"

"I have a job in Seattle."

"You have a lot more than a job here."

"You're only surmising that."

"True, but it doesn't make sense that you would leave before knowing exactly what Simon had in mind for the ranch."

"*If* he had anything in mind for the ranch." *Even if there's a will, I won't be in it.* Dena had a sudden strong impulse to explain everything to Ry, but she was so ashamed of the rebellious behavior that had caused the rift between her and her father that the impulse vanished with her next breath.

Ry's information was disturbing. She couldn't picture the ranch in the hands of a court-appointed stranger.

Neither could she imagine her father being negligent about a will. She didn't believe that she was the recipient of Simon's earthly possessions, but if there was a will, someone was. Her eyes narrowed slightly on Ry Hardin, who had finished the cookie and was dusting crumbs off his hands. Maybe Simon had left the ranch to him? Just how close had he and Ry gotten during their three-year association?

The question came out of her mouth almost as soon as it appeared in her mind. "Were you and Dad close?"

Ry gave his head a slight shake. "Not personally, no. He was my employer, and I respected his knowledge and abilities with the ranch. I believe he respected me in the same way."

"And that was the extent of your relationship?"

Ry raised an eyebrow, giving her a questioning look. "Were you thinking there was more?"

"I never thought about it one way or the other."

"Until now," Ry said softly. "Now, why would that idea even cross your mind? And what difference would it make if Simon and I had been the best of friends?"

"No difference at all," Dena answered quickly. But he was surprisingly perceptive, and she was embarrassed that he had so easily grasped the motivation behind her question. Nettie walked in then, which put an end to Dena's and Ry's conversation.

"Everyone's gone," Nettie announced, looking at the food on the table and counters. "Goodness, I won't have to do any cooking for a week."

Dena took advantage of Nettie's intrusion. "I'm going to lie down, so if you'll both excuse me..."

"Of course, honey," Nettie said sympathetically.

"Sure," Ry said. "We can talk again later."

Dena had no intention of picking up their discussion where it had left off. If her father had left the ranch to Ry, so be it. Speculation on that subject was a useless endeavor, and she wished she hadn't given Ry the impression that she was concerned about it.

But as she left the kitchen and walked down the hall to her bedroom, she knew that she was going to still be here on the fifteenth. It wasn't that she wanted the ranch for herself, but she had to know who was going to end up with it. In truth, she would much prefer Ry owning it than the state.

She prayed her father had left a will.

Dena came wide awake and was startled to see that her bedside clock flashed only 10:43 p.m. She lay there doubting that she would get back to sleep for hours, and wished that she hadn't come to bed so early in the day.

At least she had gotten through the worst of it without uncontrollable anguish, she told herself. There was an acute ache in her heart that she suspected would be there for a very long time, but she would have to learn to live with it.

"Oh, Dad," she whispered into the darkness of her room. An overwhelming sadness enveloped her. He was gone, forever out of reach. She would write no more letters and pray for an answer. She would do her job, see her friends and try to fill the void in her life with something other than the hope that would no longer be a part of her.

She would never have the chance to say, "Dad, I love you," or hear from him, "Dena, I love you now and always have. Let's forgive each other, forget the past and go on from here."

She started sobbing into her pillow, so overcome by grief and remorse that she wondered if she would ever get over it. How could he have not answered her letters? How could he have held on to anger for so long? She was his only child. Was it possible that he had never loved her?

*I can't lie here and think about it. I can't let go like this.* Throwing back her blankets, Dena jumped out of bed. Hastily she shed her nightgown and put on a sweat suit and sneakers. Then she made her way through the dark house and went outside through the back door.

The night air was cool and refreshing. She breathed in huge gulps of it. The yard lights made an after-dark stroll possible, and she began walking. There were sounds other than her footsteps and breathing—the chirping of crickets, the distant bawling of cattle, the stamping of the horses in the corrals—comforting, familiar sounds. A yellow dog that belonged to one of the men came up and sniffed her. Dena looked down at him. "Hi, boy." She kept on walking. The dog wandered off. Going beyond the glow of the yard lights, she stopped to look up at the stars. It was a beautiful night, cloudless and clear, and the millions of brightly shining stars was a moving sight.

After a few minutes, she sighed, turned back and started hiking around the lighted compound. The exercise felt good.

She'd been functioning in a fog, which was fine, as it had helped her get through the most emotionally devastating experience of her adult life, but that was over now. Her mind was clear again, and she had only herself to rely on to pick up the pieces. She would stay in Wyoming through the fifteenth, then go home.

But Seattle didn't feel like home anymore, and the ranch and Wyoming did.

"Damn," she whispered, brushing away a tear. She had cried enough for tonight.

"Dena?"

She nearly jumped out of her skin. With her heart pumping hard and fast, she turned to face the voice. Relieved to see it was only Ry, she said, "Oh, it's you. I thought everyone was sleeping."

"I think everyone else is."

"Why aren't you?"

"I'd throw that question back at you if I didn't already know the answer. I'm sorry you're having trouble sleeping, but I guess it's understandable."

"So," Dena said, "what's *your* excuse for scaring the living daylights out of me?"

"I didn't mean to scare you."

"No, well, I suppose not, but do you usually wander around in the dark?"

"It was a difficult day, Dena, not only for you."

"Are you worried about your job?" *Are you so anxious to find out if you inherited the Wind River Ranch that you can't sleep?*

"I've never had any trouble finding work, Dena. No, I'm not worried about my job."

"You strike me as the sort of man who falls asleep before his head hits the pillow, so something must be on your mind and keeping you awake."

Ry looked off into the night. "I honestly don't know what's bothering me."

Dena studied his profile. He seemed troubled, and the day *had* been difficult. As painful as it was to admit, he'd known her father better than she had. Her memories of Simon were years old; Ry's were as fresh as the night air.

Ry's gaze came around to land on her face. "You bother me."

"Me!" she exclaimed incredulously. "Why on earth would I cause you any sleeplessness?"

"Don't know. Maybe I'm worried about your attitude toward the ranch." *And maybe you've gotten under my skin for some unfathomable reason.* He'd noticed her pretty face and good figure, but only as he noticed most pretty women—impersonally. He wasn't a man to go after every attractive woman he met, and, in fact, it had been some time since he'd had any real interest in a member of the opposite sex. There were several good arguments against opening that particular door with Dena Colby. One: he suspected very strongly that she was going to be his employer. Two: she was not a naturally open and friendly person. Even in grief one's true personality came through, and Dena struck him as a loner.

And then there was the feeling in his gut that Dena harbored some sort of traumatic secret. He had no hint of what it might be, nor would he ever ask her or anyone else about it. In his book everyone was entitled to privacy. It was just that getting close to anyone with a secret was just about impossible.

Ry had questions about one thing, though. Why hadn't Dena come home and visited her father in the three years he had worked on the ranch? Why had Simon never talked about his daughter? Why had it taken Simon's death for Ry to learn that his employer even *had* a daughter?

"My attitude toward the ranch is really nobody's business," Dena said, deliberately speaking quietly as she had no desire to anger Ry. To further clarify her point on this matter, she added, "Besides, I don't know myself what I feel about it. How would you?"

"I can only go on what I've witnessed with my own eyes, Dena. I apologize if I've jumped to a false conclusion." They were near one of the corrals, and Ry leaned his back against the rails. "But the few times we've had cause to talk about it, have you shown anything but disinterest?"

"Apparently you haven't taken into consideration the fact that I had other things on my mind." This was said with some sarcasm, which Dena had not been able to forgo. "I still do," she added while her mind spun with the myriad discomfiting things yet to be faced. Maybe the worst was *not* over.

Ry was silent a moment, digested her sarcasm, decided she had a right to it and nodded. "As you said, it's none of my business. I'll try to remember that in the future." He looked up at the sky. "Nice night."

"Yes, but it's time I went in." Dena started to walk away, then stopped and turned. "Because you're the foreman and entitled to know this much at least, I've decided to stay through the fifteenth and talk to John Chandler."

"I applaud your decision," Ry said softly. "Good night."

"Good night," Dena replied, and continued on to the house.

# Four

It surprised Dena that Nettie showed no concern for the future of either the ranch or herself. The older woman went about her daily routines as always, and never once broached the subject of who was going to be running the Wind River Ranch after Dena returned to Seattle. In turn, Dena said nothing about her own concerns, as she had no answers and could see no point in causing worry over something Nettie could do nothing about.

Waiting for the fifteenth was abominable for Dena. That, coupled with the grief of losing her father and the consuming guilt and remorse over not doing more than she had about forcing a reconciliation, nearly ate her alive. To pass the time she vacuumed and dusted—every room but her father's—and got in Nettie's way in the kitchen for two days. The morning of the fourteenth, so on edge she thought she might scream, she saddled a horse and went for a ride.

Ry saw her riding away and watched her with a thoughtful expression until she was beyond the buildings and out of sight. She knew what she was doing, he decided, sitting straight and obviously in control of the animal. He needn't worry about her taking a horse out and riding alone, but it seemed that Dena was on his mind more often than not.

Two things in particular bothered him about Dena: a physical attraction he kept trying to ignore and her apathy toward the ranch. Of course, she *was* staying to talk to Chandler, so maybe she wasn't as indifferent as she acted. But Dena Colby did not share her thoughts. At least she didn't do much sharing with him. They'd spoken a few times—very briefly—since the funeral, mostly a hello in passing. His eating in the men's dining room and her eating with Nettie in the dining nook off the kitchen precluded the opportunity to talk during meals. She never sought him out to ask about ranch chores, which seemed utterly inconceivable. He and the other men could be goofing off instead of doing their jobs and she would never know. Did she honestly believe she wasn't going to inherit the ranch? Ry couldn't imagine Simon doing anything else with it, and how she could feel that way was beyond him.

*Oh, well,* he thought, returning to his work.

Dena was about a mile from the buildings when she rode to the top of a hill and stopped her horse to look back. It was a perfect seventy-five degrees, a beautiful day. The sky stretched blue from horizon to horizon. She had seen on the news that it was raining in Seattle. In fact, the whole Northwest was socked in. Wyoming summers were short, which made warm, sunny days like today extra special, and winters were a trial. But Seattle winters weren't a barrel of fun, either.

Dena felt the sting of tears and blinked them away. Letting nostalgia for her childhood home override her common sense was foolish. But she hadn't realized how much she'd missed the ranch and Wyoming. Look at the grass, the cattle, the distant buildings, she thought. Was there another place so wonderful anywhere in the world? Her roots were here, her girlhood memories. She had ridden every foot of Colby ground. She had waded in every creek and swam in the ponds, and when the ponds froze over in cold weather, she had gotten out her ice skates.

And then her mother had died and she'd started puberty,

and her moods had become erratic. Most of the time—especially around her father—she'd been resentful, hateful or weepy with self-pity. Simon had had his own problems and hadn't understood hers. As sad as it seemed now, their communication had gradually disintegrated into orders from him and sullen remarks from her.

Dena knew now that neither she nor Simon had come to terms with Opal's death. Instead of the tragedy bringing them closer together, it had caused a cataclysmic breach in their father-daughter relationship, as though each of them blamed the other for the unhappiness they both felt. If only they had been able to talk about it, Dena thought morosely. Instead, Simon had withdrawn into himself, and so had she.

If not for Nettie, Dena would not have gotten through high school. Her father's harsh insistence she attend college had been like rubbing salt into an open wound. *You're going to college, and that's that!* His unshakable attitude had only made her determined to prove him wrong.

Then she'd started dating Tommy Hogan, and Simon had really come unglued. *The Hogans are a shiftless bunch. How can you waste your time on such a boy as Tommy?*

But Tommy had been so cute, and his wisecracks and devil-may-care personality had made her laugh.

"Oh, hell," Dena groaned. Defying her father to the point of actually marrying Tommy had been a moronic, childish rebellion. If only Simon had tried talking to her in a sensible, logical manner instead of constantly laying down the law. And why hadn't she ever tried telling him how unhappy she was at home? Why had they both been so damned stubborn?

Dena rode for most of the day, questioning, thinking, shedding tears every so often. It could very well be her last opportunity to see the ranch from horseback, and she went to all of her favorite childhood haunts. It was like going back in time, as everything looked the same as the pictures she'd been carrying in her mind.

Finally, late in the afternoon, emotionally wrung out and with pangs of hunger gnawing at her empty stomach, she headed back to the compound. She had unsaddled her horse and turned the animal into a corral and was toting the saddle to the tack room when she heard men's voices in the barn.

At first she paid them no mind, but then she realized one of the voices was Ry's and that the two men were talking about women. Or one woman, at least.

"And so I been thinking 'bout getting married." That was the voice Dena couldn't connect to a face.

Dena set the saddle on a rack and went to stand just inside the door of the tack room to listen. Normally she wasn't an eavesdropper, but she couldn't help wondering which of the ranch hands was planning to get married.

"So...what d'ya think, Ry?" the faceless voice asked. Apparently the men went to Ry for advice, Dena thought. Or this one did, at least. "You were married once," the voice continued. "Should I or shouldn't I?"

Ry laughed curtly. "Jamie, I'm the wrong man to be asking about marriage. I'm not going to talk about the details of my marriage and divorce, but I will tell you that it would be a cold day in hell before I let myself get suckered into that kind of mess again. You have to make up your own mind on this, Jamie. Everyone does."

"Yeah, I guess so. But damn I'm confused. Laurie wants to get married right away, and she's really putting on the pressure. I'd like to wait a few months. I think it's the real thing, but how do you know?"

"You don't," Ry said flatly. "I doubt if anyone knows until they've been married for a while. Sorry I can't give you better advice, but that's how I feel."

In her nook behind the tack room door, Dena nodded. It was news that Ry had been married and divorced, rather interesting news. And she couldn't agree more with what he'd told Jamie. Marriage was serious business, and unless both partners actively worked at the relationship, it didn't stand a chance of survival.

Strange that she and Ry held the same philosophy regarding marriage. Well, not precisely the same. She still believed in the existence of enduring love between a man and a woman, and it didn't sound as though he did. She hadn't found it yet, and maybe she never would. But it was out there, make no mistake. She had friends in Seattle who'd been happily married for many years, couples who were still very much in love after ten, fifteen years of living together.

An impulse to show herself and tell Jamie *her* ideas about love and marriage had her taking a step through the door. But then a second impulse had her leaving the barn without saying a word. She hardly knew Jamie, just as she barely knew the other men working on the ranch, and he hadn't come to her for advice, he'd gone to Ry. Intruding on a private conversation such as they'd been having would be embarrassing for all of them.

She walked to the house and went in.

The long ride left Dena with sore muscles in her legs and back, but she felt that the discomfort was a small price to pay for seeing the ranch again, possibly for the last time. She was nervous about talking to John Chandler tomorrow, but kept her edginess to herself. After dinner, she and Nettie sat in the living room. Nettie rarely had idle hands and was knitting.

"I'm making a crib blanket for the granddaughter of an old friend who's expecting her first baby. She knows it's a girl, so, as you can see, I'm using pink yarn. Isn't it amazing that they can tell the sex of a child before it's born these days?" Nettie shook her head. "Modern technology is a marvel, isn't it?"

"Yes," Dena said quietly. She was thumbing through a magazine, registering very little of its contents. What would be Nettie's fate if the state took over the ranch? Wasn't Nettie worried about that at all? Where would she go if the state deemed she was not essential to the ranch's operation? Dena knew Nettie had no family. Her husband had died before she came to work at the ranch, and she had never had children.

But other than sorrow over Simon's death, Nettie seemed her usual contented self. Dena didn't know what to make of it, but she couldn't help worrying about Nettie's future.

The telephone rang. "I'll get it," Dena said, setting the

magazine aside and rising from her chair to go to the kitchen extension, since there was none in the living room.

"Wind River Ranch," she said into the phone.

"Is this Dena Colby?"

"Yes, it is." The male voice was unfamiliar.

"Dena, I'm John Chandler. My wife and I got home earlier today from our trip, and I just now talked to Sheila Parks, my secretary. She told me about your call to her daughter-in-law, and about your father. Dena, I can't tell you how sorry I am. Simon was such a vital man, and he was the last person I expected to…" The lawyer stopped to clear his throat. "Anyhow, since you had attempted to reach me through Sheila, I figured I should call you."

Dena's knees were suddenly weak with dread, and she sank down onto a chair. She wasn't going to have to wait until tomorrow to hear if Simon had a will; she was going to learn everything right now. "I appreciate your consideration, Mr. Chandler. Thank you for calling so soon."

"You're quite welcome, my dear, and please call me John. What was it you needed to speak to me about, Dena?"

"Why…the disposition of the ranch, of course," she stammered, startled that he would feel the need to ask such a question. "I mean, with your being Dad's lawyer, I thought you would probably know if he'd made a will."

"Are you saying you're unaware of the Colby trust?"

"I was never privy to any of Dad's business affairs, John. What kind of trust are you talking about?"

"A revocable living trust. Do you know what that is?"

"Vaguely. Actually, I'm talking *very* vaguely. I've heard the term, but that's about it."

"Okay. Let's start at the beginning. When Simon came to me about five years ago, he had an old will that he wanted updated. I'm not in favor of wills, Dena, particularly when a client has the assets Simon had. I recommended a revocable living trust instead, and after listening to an explanation of its benefits, Simon agreed."

Dena frowned. "I'm afraid I still don't understand."

"Well, simply stated, Simon was the single trustor of his

estate and you were named as the single trustee. Every asset he possessed, the ranch, the equipment, the stock, his liquid assets, everything, was put into said trust. As the sole trustee, it now belongs to you without probate. It does not eliminate inheritance taxes, but avoiding probate is a major plus in your behalf. Now, if you maintain the trust and it passes to your children, they will have to go through probate. It's all spelled out in the document, which I advise you to read. The original recorded document is in Simon's safety deposit box at the bank, but I know he kept a copy at the ranch. I'm surprised you haven't run across it.''

''I haven't gone through Dad's things,'' Dena said in a near whisper. She was having trouble believing Simon had left everything he'd owned to her. Her mind swirled with confusion. John Chandler certainly wasn't lying, so she had to believe him. But it made no sense when Simon had completely ignored her existence for seven years.

''Look, you locate the copy of the trust and read through it. Jot down any questions that might arise during the reading. Then come and see me, and we'll get everything cleared up.''

''Thank you, I will. Uh, about the checkbook...''

''Your signature isn't on file at the bank?''

''No.''

There was a moment of silence, then a small sigh from John Chandler. ''Guess I didn't know Simon as well as I thought. Can't imagine him not notifying you about the trust and seeing to the details. Well, that's neither here nor there. I'll call Lou Brock at the bank first thing in the morning and tell him you'll be coming in to file your signature.''

''Thank you.''

''Even if you have no questions after reading the trust document, drop in my office so we can meet, Dena. I'd like to remain the Colby family attorney, but that, of course, will be up to you.''

''Yes, I'll do that,'' Dena murmured. Her heart was pounding, and there was an inner trembling in her body that was almost frightening. The ranch was hers; it was too astounding to absorb without repercussion. "Goodbye, John. Thank you for calling."

She put the phone down and drew a long, shaky breath. After awhile she got up, returned to the living room and fell into a chair. "Nettie, Dad left the ranch to me."

Nettie smiled. "Well, of course he did. Did you doubt it?"

"Ardently," she said in a hoarse, shocked voice.

The following evening Dena went to the men's dining room, said hello to the five men around the table and then asked Ry to come to the office after he was through eating. His expression didn't change an iota. "I'll be there in fifteen minutes," he calmly told her, and she left the room.

"What d'ya think, Ry?" one of the men asked. "Think she found out who owns the ranch now?"

"Possibly," Ry answered. He'd heard the men talking among themselves since Simon's death, and they were all justifiably concerned about their jobs. Not that this was the only operating ranch in the country and finding another job an impossible task. But they liked working here, and Simon had always paid a good wage. Not all ranch owners did.

Dena went to the office and sat at the desk. The thick file labeled Revocable Living Trust lay before her. Last night she had looked for the copy John Chandler had said Simon kept at the ranch, found it in the file cabinet that she had never before gotten near, and set about reading it. There was more than one document pertaining to the trust, each with its own purpose, and endless copies of deeds, equipment titles and declarations of transfer. Dena had read long into the night, slept restlessly until 5:00 a.m. and got up to read everything again.

The documents themselves answered every question that arose while she read. She was now sole owner of the trust and could do with it what she wanted, including dissolution. She could also sell the trust's assets, or give them away, should she choose. Everything her father had possessed was now hers, and without probate.

She did call John Chandler about one matter: federal estate

taxes. John had explained that these taxes were based on the monetary value of an estate. The first $600,000 of an estate were exempt, but after that the tax rate was high. "I'll take care of it for you if you wish, Dena. We'll need certified appraisals of both the real and personal property, which is a simple enough step and shouldn't cost a fortune. As for filing the tax return, I'd be happy to contact the accountant in Cheyenne who has done Simon's annual income tax return for years. You haven't heard from him?"

"Not by phone," she'd said while eyeing the mail that had been stacking up since her arrival. She hadn't opened any of it and the thought of doing so now was discomfiting. The whole thing was disturbing. It was strange and probably darned peculiar of her, but yesterday while out riding she had been sentimental about the ranch and the possibility of never riding Colby ground again.

Now it was hers; she could ride Colby land every day for the rest of her life and she wasn't happy *or* sentimental about it. The responsibility was enormous. She would have to give up her nursing career to run the ranch. Her things in Seattle would have to be shipped to Wyoming. Now her sentimentality lay with the job she would have to quit, the friends she would probably never see again, her apartment and the life she had built in Seattle. Even she realized the absurdity of her unstable attitude. If she told anyone else about it, they would think her a fool. After all, how could anyone be unhappy over an inheritance such as hers?

But why had Simon executed the trust to make sure she got the ranch? The date of the documents in the file—five years previous—was during a very bad time for her. She had just divorced Tommy and was struggling to make ends meet with a minimum-wage job and nothing better on the horizon. It was about then that she began hearing the ludicrous lies the Hogans were telling about her: she'd had affairs during her marriage; she'd stolen money out of Tommy's wallet; no one could believe a word she said; poor Tommy, he'd loved and married a deceitful woman.

She had tried to talk to Simon again, panicked that he might hear those vicious stories and believe them. He'd refused to come to the phone.

And to think that while he wouldn't speak one word to her and had done everything but put it in neon to let her know she was no longer his daughter, while she had wept and suffered over those lies and the terrible mess she had made of her life, while she was reaching the decision that she had to get out of Winston and find something better than she had there, Simon had been working with John Chandler on the documents in this fat file.

Maybe that was the reason she wasn't overjoyed about inheriting the ranch. Maybe that was why she'd rolled and tossed in her bed after reading the contents of the file, and why her stomach ached now with confusion, pain and anger.

Inhaling deeply, she opened a desk drawer and slipped the file into it. It was no one else's business, and she didn't want Ry seeing it. She didn't know what she was going to do with the trust or the ranch, and she was in no mood for questions.

At least the checkbook was no longer a problem. This afternoon she had driven to Winston and gone into the bank. Mr. Brock, the bank manager, had come forward when she'd told a receptionist her name, offered condolences over Simon's death and then behaved as though she were Princess Di instead of Dena Colby. She'd understood his fawning a little better when he'd started hauling out signature cards for numerous checking and savings accounts, along with one for Simon's safety deposit box.

Unnerved because she'd believed there was only one checking account, she had left the bank without asking for account balances or peeking into the safety deposit box. Truth was, she had lived too long with a heartrending belief in her father's complete disinterest, and learning now that almost all of that time she had been a wealthy woman was distressing and, yes, even infuriating. She would have gladly forgone every penny of her inheritance if Simon had written her just one letter of forgiveness and had scrawled "Love, Dad" in closing.

Knuckles rapping on the door frame brought her out of her

painful reverie. "Ry, come in." He walked in and stood at the front of the desk. "Sit down," she said.

Ry looked at the several chairs in the room and without invitation pulled one closer to the desk. Then he sat on it, leaned back comfortably and raised his left ankle to his right knee. "What's up?" he asked while absorbing the harried expression on Dena's face. His heart sank a little. She'd discovered there was no will and she had no hold on the ranch. How sad it was to think that this beautiful ranch wouldn't stay in the Colby family. A lot of people put off making a will until it was too late, but given Simon's methodical nature as far as business went, that oversight was surprising to Ry.

His thoughts made Dena's first words a resounding shock. "I own the ranch," she said.

He couldn't believe she wasn't at least smiling. Staring incredulously at her, he blurted, "And you're not even a little bit excited about it? I wouldn't expect a person to be turning handsprings this soon after a parent's death, but owning the Wind River Ranch is worthy of a small show of excitement."

She regarded him coolly. "If you had inherited it, you'd be excited."

"Damned right. The question is, why aren't you?"

It distracted her to note that his eyes were not dark brown or black, as she'd previously thought, but a deep navy blue. In the next thought she asked herself, *so what?* And why was she even noticing the color of his eyes?

Annoyed with herself, she squirmed in her chair. "I told you about it only because as foreman you should know the ranch's status. You may pass it on to the men, if you wish."

"But you couldn't care less what they might think about it."

Dena's left eyebrow went up. "Their jobs are secure for the time being. What else *would* they think about it?"

"I only meant that it would have been a nice gesture to announce your ownership to all of us at the same time."

"A nice gesture." Dena sat there thinking over his remark, then sighed. "Ry, I'm really in no mood for nice gestures. Sorry if that disappoints you, but I never was any good at pretense and, like it or not, you're all going to have to take me as I am. Now, if you don't mind, I'd like to know of any plans Dad might have had for the ranch. The barbed wire that was delivered and sent back, for instance. Was there a specific use for that order?''

Ry was taken aback by her rather defensive self-analysis. And yet she had presented her present state of mind with such emotionless candor, his admiration for her grew and he wished he hadn't sat here and verbally picked at her lackadaisical attitude toward inheriting her father's assets. It was, after all, none of his affair, was it?

Turning his thoughts to that order of posts and barbed wire, Ry recalled telling Dena that Simon had intended to cross-fence one of the large pastures. Obviously she didn't remember his explanation. Fine. She'd been all but numb with grief, and it was a wonder any portion of the incident had registered.

"The barbed wire and posts were ordered to cross-fence a field,'' he said.

"Which field?''

There was a map, a hand-drawn rendering, of the ranch's layout tacked to the wall behind the desk. It showed signs of longtime usage, soiled in places, cracked in others. Ry got up and walked around the desk to the map. Dena swiveled her chair around, then deciding she still couldn't see the map clearly enough, got up and stood next to Ry. He pointed to a long, rectangular area. "That field," he said. Her nearness was causing a physical reaction he attempted to disregard, but her scent was in his nostrils and against his better judgment, his pulse rate was speeding up. He cleared his throat.

Dena studied the rectangle for a few moments. "In your opinion, is cross-fencing necessary?''

"Simon thought so. Since I've worked here, we've cross-fenced—'' again he pointed at the map, moving his finger to three different spots "—these pastures. It means moving the herds around more often, but it also gives relief to the grass, which makes for better growth. I can't disagree with Simon's theory, Dena, or argue with success. He was a darned good rancher.''

She was suddenly aware of how close they were to each other and took two steps back. Her putting space between them struck Ry as meaningful: she was as aware of him as a man as he was of her femaleness, and she didn't like it any more than he did. He wasn't looking for romance, especially with his employer, and obviously neither was she. To give them each more space, he returned to his chair at the front of the desk.

Dena resumed her own seat, picked up a pencil and toyed with it. She was frowning, and thinking. Ry couldn't figure out what was causing that crease in her forehead, him or the ranch, but she needn't worry about him making any moves on her, he thought grimly.

He realized he wasn't even slightly on her mind when she said abruptly, "Forget the cross-fencing. Just keep the men working at their regular jobs."

The jab he felt to his ego was astounding. Had he been *hoping* she'd been pondering her reaction to him?

"Fine," he said rather stiffly. "You're the boss now." His stomach sank when he saw the sudden tears in her eyes. He was an idiot, he thought, reminding her with a careless remark that her father was no longer around to run the ranch. But talking to her was not a simple matter. For one thing he didn't understand her. Nor did he know her. Again the question arose in his mind about why she hadn't visited the ranch in the three years he'd worked here. There was a lot more going on with Dena than met the eye, and he would like very much to know what it was.

He leaned forward with an apologetic expression. "If it was something I said, I'm sorry," he said gently.

Dena wiped her eyes with a tissue. "It's not your doing. You couldn't begin to understand."

"No argument there, but I'm a good listener, Dena."

"Maybe so, but I'm not a very good talker." Tell him everything? No, she couldn't do that, no matter how relieving it would feel to unload on someone. If she was going to do that, Nettie would be the logical person to talk to. Nettie knew it all anyhow, or most of it. But as confused and emotionally destroyed as she felt, if she tried putting her jumbled thoughts into words, even with Nettie, she would sound like a gibbering idiot.

"Um, let's see. Where were we?" she mumbled thickly, trying desperately to get ahold of herself. "Oh, yes, the fencing. Ignore it for now." Her misty eyes met Ry's across the desk. "Did you and Dad hold regular conferences on the ranch's operation?"

"Is that what you'd like the two of us to do?"

"At this point it seems sensible. Do you agree?"

"It's fine with me. Do you want me to come to the office again tomorrow evening?"

"I...guess so."

Ry got to his feet. "I'll be here. Unless we run into each other before then, I'll see you tomorrow evening." He left the office with the most awful churning in his gut. He had never been around a more unhappy person than Dena, and it made no sense. Yes, she was entitled to her period of mourning, but what he'd picked up from her in the past fifteen or so minutes was more profound and painful than ordinary grief.

Maybe it was time to ask a few questions about the Colby family. He wasn't a gossip and usually avoided people who were.

But this was different. If he was going to do Dena any good, be of any real help to her with the ranch, he had to know what was going on behind those beautiful teary eyes.

In the office, Dena laid her head back against the chair and sighed despondently. She had to make a decision about the ranch—run it herself, sell it, return to Seattle and leave it in Ry's hands—and then act upon that decision.

Why couldn't she think clearly about this, dammit, why?

# Five

The next morning Dena called Meditech in Seattle. Gail answered with a cheerful, "Good morning. Meditech Home Care, Gail speaking. How may I help you?"

"Hello, Gail, this is Dena."

"Dena! Are you home?"

"I'm still in Wyoming, Gail."

"But...your work schedule. I mean..."

"I know what you mean. I should be there and I'm not. It's a long story, Gail, but getting to the crux of it, I have to remain here for a while to settle my father's estate. Is Mr. Decker in?" Larry Decker managed the company, which was owned by a group of doctors.

"No, he had a meeting across town. You must recall the scuttlebutt about opening a second Meditech office. Well, it wasn't just rumor. It's actually under way, and I think the meeting's about that. How long do you think you'll be away?"

"I wish I knew. When I left I had no idea this would happen. I hope Mr. Decker will understand."

"If he doesn't it's his problem. People have to do what

people have to do. Look, I hate cutting this short but the other lines are lighting up like a Christmas tree. I'll pass on your message to Decker. Call in as soon as you know anything for sure, okay?"

"Will do, Gail, and thanks."

"I miss having you around, kiddo. Hope to see you soon. Bye."

"Bye," Dena said, and put down the phone.

She was sitting at her father's desk—*her* desk now, she thought with a wince—and the stack of unopened mail seemed to be glaring at her. Sighing, she pulled it closer and picked up the first envelope. Whatever decision she came to regarding the ranch, the mail could not be ignored any longer.

It proved to be a long, confusing, tiring task. First there were dozens of sympathy cards, which prompted her to remember that she must write thank-you notes to everyone who had sent flowers. And did one also send thank-you notes to those good people who had brought food to the house after the funeral? She would ask Nettie about that.

She wrote checks for the bills she readily grasped, only two, the telephone bill and the electricity bill. But there were some from vendors, and while she felt they were probably accurate, she decided to talk to Ry before paying them. Then there were letters that made her head ache. Had Simon been planning to buy more land? One letter from a Realtor gave that indication. She put the things she didn't understand in a pile so she could discuss them with John Chandler.

She was still puzzling over the mail when the phone rang. "Wind River Ranch," she said into the handset.

"This is Terry Endicott. Am I speaking to Simon's daughter?"

The voice was curt, pompous and bordering on rude. "Yes, you are," Dena said.

"Do you know who I am?"

"No, sir, I don't."

"I've been your father's accountant for a good many years, and I'd like to know why no one at the ranch had the courtesy to notify me of his death prior to his funeral. I only just learned about it a few minutes ago from John Chandler. I'm quite put out about this, Miss Colby."

"You are. Well, all I can do at this late date is apologize, Mr. Endicott, but frankly I do not feel that I have anything to apologize for. John Chandler was out of town when Dad died, and I had to wait for his return before I could even speak to him. Through him I learned that Dad's accountant lived in Cheyenne, but to tell you the truth I really didn't give a moment's thought to looking you up. Perhaps you haven't yet lost a family member, but let me tell you that it's one very overwhelming experience."

The tone of Terry Endicott's voice changed so drastically, Dena would have laughed if she'd been in a laughing mood. "Miss Colby, please forgive my bad temper. I feel as though Simon and I were far more than business associates, and it was most painful to realize I had been thinking of him as thriving and working his ranch when in fact—" Endicott stopped talking to clear his throat. "John told me he explained the technicalities of a federal tax accounting on the estate to you, and also said that he had contacted a certified appraiser. The woman's name is Ellen Clark, and I expect she will call you today or tomorrow to set up an appointment to come to the ranch."

"She may come anytime," Dena said.

"Good. Everyone concerned, especially you, I'm sure, would like to put this tedious, unpleasant task behind us as soon as possible. Since Simon was so dedicated to tying everything he owned to the Colby trust, I feel quite certain that I have current information on all of his liquid assets. However, it would be wise if you went through his papers at the ranch and his safety deposit box at the bank. We wouldn't want to miss anything and have to file an amended return somewhere down the road."

Dena's heart sank. The relatively simple chore of opening her father's mail had been traumatic; what would going through his personal papers do to her?

"All right," she said dully. "What will I be looking for?"

"Any asset that was not transferred into the trust."

Which meant comparing every deed, title, bank account and everything else she might find to the declarations of transfer in the trust file, Dena thought miserably. She didn't want to do this. She would rather take a beating than do this.

In fact she was *not* going to do it. "Mr. Endicott," she said, putting every ounce of authority she could muster into her voice, "I think that's your job. I will give you access to the safety deposit box and to the files in this house, but that's going to be the extent of my involvement in this matter. I realize it's the law and cannot be sloughed off, but I'm neither an accountant nor an attorney. I'm going to leave it all in your and John's hands, and if you don't want to comply with my wishes, I'm sure I could find an accountant who would."

"Miss Colby!" The frantic edge on the accountant's words startled Dena. "I'll be only too happy to do *whatever* you wish. As soon as Mrs. Clark turns in her appraisals, I will come out to the ranch and check Simon's files."

"Thank you," Dena said calmly. "And I'll be only too happy to take you to the bank in Winston so you may examine the contents of the safety deposit box."

"Surely you've already done so."

"No, sir, I haven't, nor do I have any desire to do so. Was there anything else, Mr. Endicott?"

"Uh, no, not for the moment. I'll stay in touch."

"Do that. Goodbye."

Feeling drained, Dena set down the phone then put her head in her hands. She had never talked to a businessperson the way she had to Terry Endicott, demandingly, threateningly. It was a bitter-tasting proof that she was a different woman than she'd been before the inheritance, proof that money gave one a sense of power, even though she had no accurate idea of the value of the trust. However, Endicott had proved it himself by kowtowing to her demands with no more than a pleading whimper. Asserting herself in a you'll-do-it-my-way-or-else manner had caused the bluster he'd called with to evaporate like an ice cube under a hot sun.

Dena groaned out loud. How in God's name was she going to live through this and remain sane? No one had said how long the paperwork would take, but she unhappily suspected it was going to be months. And every day there was a new player—John Chandler, Terry Endicott, a woman named Ellen Clark.

Then something Gail had said flashed into her mind. *People have to do what people have to do.* It wasn't any great pearl of wisdom, but she embraced it because it seemed to fit her situation and made her feel a little better.

Reaching for the phone again, she dialed John Chandler's number. She might as well ask him about those perplexing letters and get them out of the way.

Ry spotted Nettie carrying a small sack out to the trash bin. Loping across the compound from the barn, he called her name.

She gave him a backward glance and continued on to the bin, which was where he caught up with her. "You need me for something, Ry?" she asked.

"Just some conversation, Nettie." He looked away from her sharp, curious eyes for a moment, then brought his gaze back to her. "I have some questions about Dena. Would you mind answering them?"

"If you have questions about Dena, why not ask her?"

"Dena's not an easy woman to talk to."

"And I am?" Nettie said pertly.

Ry couldn't help grinning. "Don't know. We've never done much talking, have we?"

"Not much," Nettie agreed. "Go ahead and ask your questions, but remember that my loyalties have been with the Colbys for a good many years now."

"I understand. Nettie, why didn't Dena come home while Simon was still alive?"

Nettie's expression became a bit wry. "You do get right to the heart of a matter, don't you? Before I tell you anything, you have to give me a darned good reason why I should."

Ry stood there and thought. A good reason for asking questions. Nettie was a feisty little lady and had no qualms about putting him on the spot. Of course, he'd started this, hadn't he?

"I have only one reason, Nettie," he said soberly. "The future of this ranch. Dena doesn't seem to give a damn about it. Cutting it even closer, I think she resents inheriting it. Now maybe she has cause for feeling that way, but if that's the case, didn't Simon know about it? He loved this ranch, Nettie, and why would he leave it to someone who doesn't?"

Nettie removed her eyeglasses and wiped the lenses on a corner of her apron. "Are you planning to stay on as fore-man?"

"As long as there's a job here, I'll be here, too."

Nettie put her glasses back on and sighed. "Simon did love this place, Ry. But you're wrong about Dena's feelings toward it. Her resentment isn't caused by the ranch, it's because of…oh, dear, I don't know if I should be talking about this. It's really none of my business, you know."

Ry frowned. "Nettie, please. All I want to do is help. Anything you tell me will not be repeated to another living soul. You have my word on that."

"Help. Yes, Dena could use some help. Not that every man working here isn't earning his pay, but you're not talking about that kind of help, are you?"

"No," Ry said quietly. "I guess what I'd like to do is go the extra mile to keep this ranch on line. Do whatever it takes. But I feel as though I'm on the outside looking in, or trying to look in. Dena's a closed book, Nettie. Last night in the office I realized that her lack of spirit isn't all due to grief. There's something else bothering her, isn't there?"

"Oh, it's grief, all right, but it's not all because of Simon's death. You see…" Again Nettie stopped. The expression on her face told Ry that she was having a hard time with this.

"Nettie, I know you're not a gossip, and I know you're a decent, hardworking, loyal woman. But can you, in all good conscience, stand by and do nothing to pull Dena out of the doldrums in the name of loyalty?" He was grasping at straws, willing to use any argument to get Nettie to open up, because now he knew without a doubt that *she* knew what Dena's problem was.

"It's possible that time will take care of everything," Nettie said, speaking uneasily.

"Anything's possible, Nettie. It's possible that Dena might decide to sell the ranch."

"Sell it! Land's sake, Simon would spin in his grave. And so would her mother." Nettie's eyes narrowed on Ry. "Did she mention selling to you?"

"No, but when someone's so obviously unhappy, don't they usually try to get away from the cause? Don't forget, Nettie, she's a registered nurse. Maybe she's missing her job."

Nettie waved that idea away. "She'd be just as unhappy in Seattle, and I think she's smart enough to know it. Okay, I'm going to tell you what's going on, and I expect you to keep your word about not repeating the story."

"I swear it, Nettie."

"It's hot here in the sun. Let's go sit under the trees."

Ry followed her to a shaded area with three redwood chairs. Simon had often sat out here on summer evenings, sometimes alone, sometimes with Nettie or one of the men. Ry had joined him on occasion, but they had never talked about anything other than the ranch. He wondered, as he seated himself in the chair next to the one Nettie chose, what Simon and Nettie had talked about.

Nettie looked at the house. "Did you know Dena was married once?"

"No, I didn't. What happened?"

"She got a divorce. It only lasted a couple of years." Nettie sniffed. "It's a wonder it lasted that long." Her gaze swung to Ry. "Tommy Hogan's a deadbeat. His whole family is a worthless bunch. Oh, yes, he's still in the neighborhood. Came to the house the day of the funeral, in fact. Walked right up to Dena as though she should be glad to see him. He doesn't have two quarters in his jeans, but he's got gall. I'll give him that. Anyway, he's what started the trouble," Nettie added.

"The marriage or the divorce?"

"The marriage. Well, it wasn't really the start of the trouble, but it was the final straw for Simon. After Opal, Dena's mother, died, something went wrong. Simon never got over losing his wife, and Dena turned into a brat. I love her dearly and always have, but I can't think of a better word than *brat* for the way she behaved. She defied her father in every way a young girl can and still remain living at home. More than once I wanted to slap her sassy mouth, I don't mind admitting, but that wasn't Simon's way. He just kept getting quieter and more withdrawn, and the quieter he got, the louder Dena got. Those were not good years.

"She dated some in high school," Nettie continued after a pause. "Nothing was said about that until she started going out with Tommy Hogan. Like many of the people around here, Simon had no respect for the Hogan clan. He said so one night, and the fight was on. I honestly think Dena would have lost interest in Tommy if Simon hadn't voiced his opinion so strenuously."

"So she married Tommy to spite her father?"

Nettie sighed. "What do I know? Maybe she loved him, or imagined herself in love with him. He's good-looking, and young girls are so foolishly susceptible to good looks. Anyhow, Simon had always intended for Dena to go to college. He wanted her to pick a good school, and was prepared to pay for every cent of the cost of her education. She came home one night just before high school graduation and announced that she and Tommy were getting married. I thought Simon would either pass out or explode. You should have seen his face, poor man. It was one terrible blow, I can tell you."

Ry nodded thoughtfully. This was all very interesting, but what did it have to do with Dena's present attitude? So what if she'd married a jerk? She'd wised up and gotten rid of him, and now apparently had a good career in Seattle. Ry still felt her melancholy, gloom-and-doom disposition had something to do with Seattle. Inheriting the ranch had virtually trapped her in Wyoming, after all.

Nettie went on. "They argued for days about it, but neither would give an inch. I stayed out of it because I loved them both. But I felt Dena was making a horrible mistake. Believe me, Tommy Hogan was no substitute for a college education. And she was so young, Ry, just eighteen. Anyway, she packed her clothes and personal possessions. Tommy was waiting for her in his rundown old car. I could see him through the living room window, chain-smoking cigarettes and tossing the butts out on the ground.

"Simon came in and saw the suitcases and boxes. 'You're really going to do this?' he asked Dena. 'Yes,' she said with fire in her eyes, just daring him to try to stop her. I know if he hadn't been the stoic, stalwart man he was that he would have broken down and cried. Instead he told her, 'If you go through with this, if you marry Tommy Hogan, I will never speak to you again.'"

"Oh, it was an awful moment, Ry. I knew he meant what he'd said, and I thought my heart would break on the spot. Dena tossed her head disdainfully and began hauling her things out to the car. Tommy kept his distance, believe me. He never even set foot on the porch, the danged coward. But he loaded her boxes and suitcases into the trunk and back seat of his car, and away they went."

Ry had become incredulous. "Are you saying that Simon kept his word and never spoke to Dena again?"

"That's exactly what I'm saying," Nettie said sadly. "She and Tommy lived in Winston, and she drove out here several times. Whenever she walked into the house Simon would walk out. She was growing up fast—the reality of a bad marriage was hitting her right between the eyes, and I don't think she had believed her dad when he'd sworn to never speak to her again. She left here in tears more than once, I can tell you."

Nettie sighed. "Then there was the divorce and finally her move to Seattle. She phoned often during that period and Simon never once took a call. When she was situated in Seattle she started writing letters. I don't know what Simon did with them—probably burned them—but I know Dena never got one from him. She and I kept in touch. She was obsessed with earning her father's forgiveness and one day reconciling with him." Nettie sighed again. "Simon never once mentioned her name after she left with Tommy that day. And he gathered up

all of the photos of her scattered throughout the house and did
something with them. I honestly don't know if he packed them
away or destroyed them.''

"My God," Ry mumbled. He'd known Simon had been a
hard, stern man, but to disown your only child for marrying
someone you didn't like, or even thought unworthy, was the
most cruel, unreasonable thing he'd ever heard of. Then he
remembered the ranch. "But he left her the ranch. If he was
so dead set against her, if he had no feelings for her, why did
he leave everything he'd created in his lifetime to her?''

"Ry, he had feelings for her. I think he suffered every day
of his life after she left. But he'd sworn not to ever speak to
her again, and he was too darned stubborn to swallow his pride
and admit he loved and needed her.

"Besides, she paid plenty for her defiance, and he had to
know that as well as I did. There was a lot of talk after that
divorce, and I don't see how he could have avoided hearing
some of it.''

"What kind of talk?''

"A lot of lies and vicious rumors, instigated, I'm sure, by
the Hogans," Nettie said disgustedly. "Well, that's the whole
awful story. She's being eaten alive by guilt and remorse. Can
you blame her for not being thrilled about inheriting the ranch?
She never expected that to happen, you know. I did, but she
didn't.''

"No," Ry said quietly, "I can't blame her for not being
thrilled." It occurred to him that Nettie could have abbreviated
the story to a few simple sentences: *Simon and Dena had a
falling out years ago. They never reconciled. Inheriting the
ranch was an unexpected shock.*

But maybe Nettie had needed to tell it all. Ry doubted that
she'd ever told anyone else what she knew about the breach
between father and daughter. He would definitely keep his
word about not repeating it to anyone. Deep down he wished
that he'd kept his nose out of Dena's business. What he'd
heard from Nettie was damned disturbing, and he knew it was
going to bother him till his dying day, whether he was on the
Wind River Ranch or in Timbuktu.

He got to his feet. "Thanks for talking to me, Nettie. I'd better get back to work now."

Nettie got up, too. "Do you feel any better now that you know it all?"

He looked away. "No. It wasn't what I expected to hear."

Nettie nodded wisely. "Wasn't it curiosity that killed the cat?" She patted Ry on the arm. "At least you'll understand Dena's moods better. And I'm very glad to know how much you want to help her. You know what I think would help most? Getting her to talk about it."

"Without letting on that I know her history? I don't think that's possible, Nettie."

Nettie hesitated, then sighed. "I suppose you're right. Well, do what you can."

"Yes, ma'am. See you later." Ry walked off toward the barn. He'd heard some sad stories in his time, but none to compare with Dena's. No wonder she walked around looking like the last rose of summer.

On the other hand, how much sass and defiance could a parent take from a kid?

While the men were having their evening meal, Dena hurried through her own dinner and went to the office to wait for Ry. Everything—the ranch, the trust, the mail, the telephone conversations with John Chandler, Terry Endicott and the appraiser, Ellen Clark—seemed like monumental problems she didn't want to deal with. Within that troubling, unstable morass was one solid piece of humanity—Ry Hardin.

It had occurred to Dena at some point of the unnerving day that Ry could take the notion to leave the ranch. Yes, he had said he would stay as long as she needed him, but people changed their minds over the smallest things. It made her sick to her stomach to picture herself floundering with the ranch without Ry. She ached for reassurance but worried how he might react to her bringing up the subject and attempting to extract an unbreakable promise from him. In fact, she would like to go so far as to suggest something in writing between them.

But she didn't know Ry well enough to predict his response to a request for a contract of employment. She would settle for just hearing him say it again, she decided uneasily. Perhaps she could subtly manipulate their conversation this evening so that he would say again that she could count on him. It would give her immeasurable comfort.

*Oh, God,* she thought miserably. How had her life come to this? *Dad, is this your revenge?* One would think—an outsider, in particular—that growing up on a ranch would prepare a person for taking over the reins. But she'd never paid the slightest bit of attention to the business end of her home. Why, instead of wallowing in self-pity after her mother died, hadn't she gotten involved in the ranch's operation? If nothing else, it might have put her and her father on better terms. And certainly, any knowledge and experience she would have picked up would be of great benefit now.

Dena sighed dismally. If only it were possible to change the past.

Ry rapped on the woodwork. "Ready for me?"

His abrupt intrusion on Dena's self-possessed thoughts flustered her. Jumping up, she proclaimed, "Yes, of course. Come in."

Ry ambled into the room nonchalantly, doing his level best to appear the same as he had last night in this same situation. But exactly how *had* he appeared to Dena? She'd told him about her ownership of the ranch, and he'd rudely told her she should be excited about it. She probably thought of him as an insensitive oaf.

They sat in the same chairs they'd used the night before. Ry saw the same harried expression on her face. Other than different clothing and date on the calendar, tonight felt like last night.

But while Dena was the same, he wasn't. He could put on a false face and pretend nothing had changed in the last twenty-four hours, but it had. Nettie was right. The best therapy anyone could give Dena to help her move past her guilt would be to get her to talk about it.

"So," he said casually, "how was your day?"

She blinked in surprise. "Pardon?" She'd heard him, but his question was so unexpected that she'd reacted like a total dunce. He sounded and looked friendly, and she hadn't been thinking of him as a friend. A valued employee, yes, but not a friend. Maybe he *did* plan on sticking around.

"I asked how your day went."

If he was offering friendship, she certainly was going to accept it. Lord knew she could use a friend about now, and what better way to cement a relationship? Even an employer-employee relationship.

She drummed up a smile. Not a wide, carefree smile, but a smile nonetheless. "It was a difficult day," she said. Why lie about it, or gloss it over? "I feel rather smothered by paperwork that I don't comprehend, to be honest." She shoved the small stack of unpaid invoices she'd set aside for this evening across the desk. "These, for example. Would you mind taking a look at them? They're probably accurate billings, but I'd like your input before paying them."

"Sure, I'll look at them. Glad to." Ry picked up the invoices and began going through them.

Dena sat back in her chair and regarded him thoughtfully, realizing that the more she saw of him, the better looking he became. He was not a flirtatious man, rather serious, in fact. Mature, she thought, a grown-up who'd been through a bad marriage and divorce, like herself. He did have a marvelous body, she thought next, startling herself with the observation while staring at his broad shoulders and splendid chest. But there was more to admire about him than his physique. Apparently he was a steady, reliable person, a dependable man. He'd worked here for three years, and why would he wander off now? Why, in heaven's name, had she tortured herself most of the day with visions of him leaving her alone with the ranch?

Ry laid the invoices back on the desk. "They're all legit. Go ahead and pay them."

Dena nodded. "Thank you, I will."

"You know, I understand your aversion to paperwork. Never liked dealing with it myself."

"Have you ever *had* to deal with it? I mean, sometimes we're forced into situations…" Remembering that last night he had said quite plainly that she should be excited about inheriting the ranch, she stopped in mid-sentence, fearing she was sounding like a complainer. What she needed to do was expand their budding friendship, not bore him with complaints neither of them could do anything about.

She *did* feel trapped, Ry thought empathetically. Even though the ranch was worth a small fortune, she would rather be in Seattle. What a tragic conclusion to teenage defiance and parental strictness. Had Simon planned to one day forgive her youthful indiscretions? Surely he hadn't thought he would die so young. Tragic, all of it.

"Listen," he said on impulse. "How about forgetting paperwork tomorrow and tagging along with me? I'll be on horseback most of the day, checking the herds and pastures. It'll get you out of the house and maybe give you a better idea of what the men and I are doing to earn our pay."

"I'm sure you're all earning your pay." Tag along with Ry all day? Ride beside him on Colby land and hear his opinion on various aspects of ranching? She could ask questions and learn a lot, and even if they didn't speak a word it was a wonderful idea. For the first time since Ry had called her with the news of her father's death, Dena felt a glimmer of excitement.

Ry grinned. "We are," he said, "but wouldn't you like to see it for yourself?"

After a long breath, Dena smiled. "Yes, I really would. Thank you for the invitation. What time should I be ready in the morning?"

"Around seven. That'll get breakfast out of the way and give me time to talk to the men about work assignments." Ry got up. "You know, Dena, the worst of what you're going through will pass in time. Try not to dwell on the past. Look ahead instead of behind you. My belief is that there are darned few people who get through life without some sort of trauma." He smiled. "See you in the morning."

Dena sat there long after he'd gone, puzzling over his advice. He couldn't possibly know about the old problems between Simon and herself, could he? Dena's heart skipped a beat. If he did know, why not come right out and say so? Oh, Lord, what if he'd heard the awful gossip and lies the Hogans had circulated about her? What if he believed them?

She suddenly felt choked by her own breath. Ry knew something, and it wasn't at all comforting to realize that she was as ashamed of the truth as she was humiliated by the lies. Tears filled her eyes. How could they ever be friends with that between them?

# Six

There really was no debate in Dena's mind about whether she should or should not go with Ry on his daily rounds because he might have heard some less than admirable information, true or not, about her past. He was trying to be nice, and she wasn't going to permit pride to ruin a possible friendship with a man she desperately needed at the ranch. Besides, she truly wanted a day on horseback. She loved riding and knew that it was something she should do often while the weather was still good.

Weather aside, she should ride as much as possible while she was here, she thought with a bit of a scowl. "Darn," she mouthed under her breath. No matter what subject came to mind, it always led her back to her indecisiveness with the ranch.

But she was not going to let it ruin her day, she thought with a determined thrust of her chin. Dressed and ready at six-thirty, she went to the kitchen for some breakfast. The men had already eaten, and Nettie was loading the large commercial dishwasher that serviced the ranch's needs. "Good morning, Nettie."

Nettie looked up. "Morning, honey. You must be going riding."

It was obvious from Dena's boots, jeans and the hat she was carrying that she wasn't going to spend the day in the office. "Ry suggested last night that I tag along with him today," she explained. "Frankly, I jumped at the chance to see the ranch through his eyes. I'm hoping to learn a few things. It's hard to believe how limited my knowledge is about the ranch's operation."

"Well, I'm glad to see you getting out of the house, whatever your reasons. How about some pancakes? There's batter left from the men's breakfast."

"Pancakes would be great, but I can fix them. You go ahead and finish with the dishwasher."

"No, you pour yourself a cup of coffee and sit down. I'll have those pancakes ready in two shakes of a lamb's tail." Nettie switched on the griddle to heat.

Dena couldn't help a smile. The kitchen was Nettie's personal property, and she didn't like other people messing it up. The times that Dena had tried to help with the cooking since she got home had made Nettie so nervous, she'd become all thumbs.

"Okay, if that's what you prefer," Dena agreed. With a mug of coffee, she sat on a stool at the counter. "Nettie, I'm expecting a woman named Ellen Clark to call. She's an appraiser, and needs to assess the value of the ranch and equipment."

Nettie frowned and spoke uneasily. "Dena, I hope you're not thinking of selling out."

The remark startled Dena. Selling was one of her options, but she didn't want Nettie worrying about it. If she did sell, she would see to it that Nettie received a lifetime income from the proceeds, but it wasn't something she was prepared to discuss with anyone at this point. She had a lot to wade through before she made a decision about the ranch, and it was a doubly difficult determination because every aspect of that decision was so intermingled with emotion.

"The appraisal is strictly for estate tax purposes, Nettie," Dena said quietly. "Requested by John Chandler and Terry Endicott so they may comply with federal tax law."

"Oh," Nettie said, obviously relieved. After testing the temperature of the griddle with a few drops of water, she ladled batter onto it, making three perfect circles.

"Anyhow, if Mrs. Clark calls for an appointment, tell her she may come to the ranch at her convenience. I can't see any reason why I would have to be here, so if she wants to come today, fine." Actually, Dena would be relieved if Ellen Clark made her appearance while she was gone. If the woman had questions, it was doubtful Dena would be able to answer them, so it was best if she got her answers from John or Terry.

"If she calls, I'll tell her what you said," Nettie promised. She glanced out the window. "It looks like we're in for another sunny day. Lovely day for a ride."

"Appears so," Dena agreed. The weather had been so great since she'd come home that Dena expected to wake up to gray skies every morning. She watched as Nettie expertly flipped the pancakes, and for some reason became very melancholy. "Mother was very relieved when you came to the ranch, wasn't she?"

"Your mother couldn't do the cooking and cleaning any longer."

"I know, but you fit in so perfectly, Nettie. How did Dad find you?"

"Simple. He put an ad in the paper and I answered it." Nettie transferred the three pancakes from the griddle to a plate and brought it to the counter. "Do you want butter?"

"Just syrup, Nettie, thanks." She'd started avoiding fat several years prior, and had discovered that pancakes tasted just fine without butter.

Dena began eating. "Would you have answered that ad if you'd known what you were getting into?"

Nettie removed her glasses to wipe them on her apron. "Dena, I was a very lonely woman when I answered that ad.

My husband had died three years before, and I was getting awfully tired of talking to myself. Oh, I had some good friends—still do—but even the best of friends don't replace family. In my opinion, anyway." She put the glasses back on her face. "You see, Dena, what I found here was family. I hope you don't object to my thinking of you as family—just as I did your mother and father—but..."

"Object!" Dena got off her stool and hurried around the counter to hug Nettie. "You *are* family," she said with a tremble in her voice and tears in her eyes. "The only family I have."

Nettie teared up, too, and their embrace went on for several emotional moments. When they separated, both wiped their eyes and smiled.

"To answer your question," Nettie said, "yes, I would have called on that ad even if I'd been able to predict the future."

"I regret so many things," Dena said sadly.

"I know you do, honey."

"I wish Dad had known how much I've changed."

Nettie sighed. "Your father was a good man, Dena. But when he said something, he stuck by it. I wish he would have given you some kind of break, too. He hurt himself as much as he did you with that old grudge, and it's strange that he didn't realize it."

"He carried that grudge too far, Nettie."

Nettie sighed again. "I know, honey, I know." After a pause Nettie said, "Finish your pancakes, Dena. And you'd better take some sandwiches along for lunch. Ry's a hard worker, and if you're going to be following him around, you might be out all day. I'll make some nice beef sandwiches from that roast we had last night. You eat."

Dena returned to her stool and picked up her fork. Nettie went to the refrigerator and brought out the leftover roast. "Dena, have you given any thought to your father's personal possessions?" Nettie asked.

Dena slowly lowered her fork. "Yes, of course."

"I'm not trying to push you into anything, but someone's going to have to go through his clothes and such."

"I...I can't go into his bedroom, Nettie," Dena said in a low, taut voice. "Not yet."

"Well, I guess there's no rush," Nettie hastened to reply. "Forget I mentioned it."

Dena pulled on her riding gloves as she walked to the barn. There was a strap over her right shoulder, supporting the canvas bag in which Nettie had put the sandwiches and a canteen of water. The hat on Dena's head shadowed the frown between her eyes. Someone did have to go through her father's things, and that someone should be her. She could probably talk Nettie into taking care of the emotionally devastating task, but it wouldn't be a fair request at all. No, this was something she couldn't demand someone else see to, as she'd done with Terry Endicott and Simon's files and safety deposit box. But Lord only knew when she'd work up the courage to even enter that bedroom, let alone go through her father's bureaus and closet.

Ry was waiting with two saddled horses. "Morning," he called when he saw her coming.

"Good morning," she returned as she walked up to the horses and Ry.

"I saddled the same horse you used the other day. Hope that's okay."

"It's fine. She's a nice little mare with good manners. Does she have a name?" Dena petted the mare's nose.

"Goldie."

Dena smiled. "Well, Goldie, we got along just fine before, didn't we? I'm sure today will go as well." Turning to Ry, she slid the strap of the bag from her shoulder. "Nettie insisted I take some lunch along."

Ry grinned. "Enough for two?"

"More than enough."

"Great. We'll have a picnic somewhere along the line. Ready to go?"

Dena secured the canvas bag over the saddle horn, winding the strap around it several times so the bag wouldn't be bumping her leg all day. "All set."

They mounted. Dena squirmed a little to settle herself in the saddle. Ry had immediately nudged his horse into a walk and didn't look back. Dena clicked her tongue and flapped the reins. "Okay, Goldie, let's go."

They had been riding for hours. Ry had located each of the men at his job for the day and talked to them for a few minutes. Now they just seemed to be meandering and chatting, which Dena was thoroughly enjoying.

"As I'm sure you know, there are about two thousand head of cattle on the ranch at the present," Ry said. Dena didn't know, but she said nothing about her lack of knowledge. "The overall herd runs close to that number every summer, then is brought down to about half that figure by the fall sale, give or take a few hundred head. The current year's calves are kept for at least a year, sometimes two. Depends a lot on whether they're male or female. Simon always maintained enough females to replenish the herd each year. The steers are the main cash crop, of course."

"Do we still use bulls, or do we impregnate with artificial insemination now?" Dena asked.

"Both. The bulls take care of the cows we miss with AI."

"And how many bulls do we have?"

"Four. We'll start AI in another few weeks, and turn the bulls into the cows' pastures about three weeks after that. I'm sure I don't have to explain animal husbandry to you, but any cow already impregnated won't let a bull get near her. 'Course, the bulls don't pick up the right scent from pregnant cows, so they don't waste their time chasing after them."

Dena smiled at the visual. When she'd lived on the ranch it had all been done with bulls, and mating season had been wild. She had learned very young what made baby cows, and had taken the process in stride. She'd been in her early teens before she associated the mating of cattle to human procreation, and had accepted it as naturally as breathing.

She changed the subject. "I noticed on my previous ride the many small herds. It looked to me about a hundred head to a herd."

"Right on," Ry concurred. "And we keep moving them from one pasture to another to preserve the grass. Did you see the hay fields?"

"I think so."

"Well, they should be greener than they are. This weather is great for humans, but not so good for dry-land hay. The area really needs a good drenching." Ry turned his head to look at Dena. "You know, I never could figure out why Simon didn't irrigate. A system would be easy to put in, and shouldn't be too costly. It sure would produce a lot more hay. I doubt that the ranch would have to spend a dime buying anyone else's hay for winter feeding if we irrigated the alfalfa fields. In the long run, it would save the ranch money."

"Well, it's certainly something to think about," Dena murmured. She knew why her father hadn't put in an irrigation system. He'd ranched one way all his life, and had never spent money on uncertainties. The ranch had prospered without irrigation, and it would have made no sense to Simon to change his ways just because someone else thought he should. She didn't ask Ry if he'd talked to Simon about irrigation, because she knew he had and Simon had completely disregarded the idea.

Bitterness overtook her suddenly. No one had ever told Simon Colby what to do, had they? He'd been a stubborn, mean-minded, know-it-all man, and her longtime heartache was proof of his inability to admit he hadn't been right about everything. How could he not have answered her letters, her desperate telephone calls? She had always accepted full blame and responsibility for their breach, but now, for the first time really, she felt anger. It had all been so damned senseless. Yes, she'd behaved badly after her mother's death, but so had Simon. And he'd never just talked to her, not about the ranch, not about anything. She'd felt so alone. Without Nettie she *would* have been alone.

"It's getting close to noon. How about eating our lunch at the spring?"

"Fine with me," Dena agreed. It was so pleasant walking her horse through the fields that she didn't care in which direction Ry took her. Birds sang, the sun was bright and warm, and the beauty wherever she looked was mood elevating. A sudden fierce sense of ownership startled her. This was *her* land, *her* grass and animals. Why it was hers was a nebulous question, but hers it was. Had Simon thought past her to future generations? Had he hoped she would one day have children and pass the trust and its assets on to them? The Colby name would be lost somewhere along the line, but Colby blood would still possess this beautiful land. It was a logical explanation as to why a father who had disowned his daughter would leave her what he'd loved most, but it was not emotionally satisfying for Dena. In fact, it aroused bitter feelings and another spurt of anger. The perfect revenge for her father's cruel disregard for so many years would be to sell everything and leave Wyoming forever.

Dena let Goldie fall back behind Ry's horse, and for several minutes enjoyed a perverse pleasure in envisioning revenge, something that had never so much as entered her mind before. She had never sought vengeance for Simon's harsh attitude. She'd wept and berated herself, she'd written pleading letters and spent more money than she could afford on long-distance calls to the ranch, and she'd lived for years with an overload of guilt and remorse. But not once had she plotted or prayed for revenge.

She gave her head a quick shake to clear it. What was wrong with her, thinking of such a terrible thing? How would selling the Wind River Ranch hurt her father now? How could anything she do hurt him now? Or please him? *Wake up and smell the coffee*, she angrily told herself. *No one other than Nettie gives a damn* what *you do.*

That was her fault, too. Oh, a few female friends might be glad if she returned to Seattle, but there certainly wasn't a man waiting and worrying about her. She thought of her life in Seattle, and how many times she had refused one-on-one invitations from men. She'd gone out socially in groups on occasion, but in all the years since her divorce she had not met one man who had aroused any interest beyond friendship, and even that was rare.

Did she blame all men for Simon's and Tommy's sins? My Lord, was she that petty?

Dena sighed as the anger drained from her system to be replaced by self-reproach. It always came back to that, didn't it? If she felt anger or resentment one second, she switched to self-condemnation in the next. It was because she had loved her father so much, and he hadn't loved her at all. Tears filled her eyes.

Furtively Dena pulled a tissue from her pocket and wiped the telltale moisture from under her dark sunglasses. She didn't want Ry seeing her weepy and emotional ever again. He was a steady, rugged, salt-of-the-earth kind of man, and she wanted to appear as strong as he was. Prove to him that she could take it on the chin.

Riding behind him gave her the opportunity to study him without his knowledge. His broad back was an appealing sight, she thought, then frowned a little because she wasn't accustomed to mentally measuring the width of a man's shoulders. But that one small bit of admiration led her deeper into unfamiliar territory. Ry was really quite good-looking. Would she have noticed that sooner under ordinary circumstances? He had the rugged good looks of a man who had worked outdoors all his life. Furthermore, he emanated a confidence that gave Dena the impression he knew exactly what he wanted out of life.

She envied that sort of confidence. Her own had apparently been left in Seattle when she'd boarded the plane for Wyoming, as she had never lacked confidence in her nursing career and now felt completely devoid of the trait. She honestly hoped Ry didn't think of her as a helpless, emotional female or an inept employer, but had he seen any other side of her? It really was time to shape up, wasn't it? No one could eradicate her emotional scars, not even she had the power to do that. But she could stop dwelling on them nearly every minute of every day, couldn't she?

"The spring's just ahead," Ry called over his shoulder.

She knew precisely where the spring was, just as she knew the location of each and every other landmark on the ranch.

She could have pointed that out to Ry, but all she said was, "I see it."

Ry reined his horse in so she could catch up with him. He wasn't looking at her, however. "You can also see from here some of the erosion caused by heavy runoffs in past years. Right now the runoff is about normal, but even so there's several ponds. The cattle drink from those ponds when they're pastured in this area, but think what that water could do for the hay fields."

Side by side again, they rode closer to the spring and adjacent ponds. "You seem rather passionate about an irrigation system," Dena said.

"It only makes sense, Dena."

"Perhaps," she said. But there was no commitment in her voice, and Ry realized she had no real interest in this subject. He changed it.

"Are you ready to eat now?" he asked.

"Yes," she said. "Let's have lunch under those cottonwoods on the other side of the spring."

They circled their horses to the trees, dismounted and tethered the animals on the edge of the grove so they could nibble at the grass growing there. Dena carried the canvas lunch bag, and she and Ry found a shady spot. "This will do nicely," she said, wincing a little as she sank to the ground.

"Sore muscles?" Ry asked, lowering himself as he spoke.

Dena began digging out the sandwiches. "I expected it. Here you go." She passed him a foil-wrapped sandwich.

"Thanks."

A lovely tranquillity descended upon Dena as they ate their simple fare. She wondered about the sensation, wondered why in this spot—pretty as it was—and with this man, she should feel so at peace. If she could only preserve the feeling, she thought with a small sigh. If she could hold it in her heart for the rest of her days, she would die a contented woman.

But it lasted only a few minutes and reality returned. She looked at Ry, who appeared completely relaxed as he finished the last of his sandwich. Questions suddenly arose in her mind. "Were you and...Dad friends?"

Ry's eyes met hers. She had brought up this subject before, but apparently he hadn't satisfied her curiosity. "I don't think I would categorize our relationship that way. Why do you ask?"

"Just conversation, I guess. Are you friends with the other men?"

"We're friendly, if that's what you mean."

"They can talk to you, come to you for advice on personal matters?" She was remembering the conversation she'd overheard between him and Jamie.

"It happens," Ry said.

"But you couldn't go to Dad for personal advice."

"I never tried it, Dena. Never needed any advice on 'personal matters,' as you put it."

"But you do have a personal life, don't you? I mean, your entire existence couldn't possibly revolve around the ranch."

Ry took off his hat, laid it on the ground, then stretched out full-length and used the hat for a pillow. "I like this ranch, Dena," he said, sounding as contented as he looked. "I don't leave it very often."

"Do you wish it were yours?"

He cast her a surprised glance. "I've never thought about it."

"Really? You're obviously very knowledgeable about raising cattle, and I can't help wondering why you don't have a ranch of your own."

Ry got comfortable again. He closed his eyes. "I had one once. It was my folks' place in Texas, and after they died it belonged to my two sisters and myself. My sisters are older than me and had already married and left home. Weren't at all interested in keeping the old homestead, and they voted to sell it. I hung on for a while, arguing with them about it, but what the heck? Was anything worth causing a breach in the family? I didn't think it was, so we sold out and everyone was happy."

"Then you're close to your sisters."

"I'd say so."

"But you would have preferred keeping your family ranch."

"For a while, yes. Ended up with a nice bank account, though, and I could have bought another place. Still could."

Dena's heart skipped a beat. She needed Ry here. At least she needed him here for as long as she stuck around herself. "Are you looking for one?" she asked, concealing her nervousness about this topic behind a passive expression.

"Not actively."

Dena breathed a small sigh of relief. "Why did you leave Texas and come to Wyoming?"

With his eyes still closed, Ry smiled. "You're sure full of questions today. I just sort of drifted north, Dena, looking around, seeing country I'd heard about all my life. I liked Wyoming right away, and I drove some back roads and stopped at ranches just to see them."

"With the possibility of purchase in the back of your mind?"

"Sometimes. Anyhow, I was in Winston having lunch at the Chuckwagon Café when I heard a couple of guys talking about the Wind River Ranch. The name struck my fancy, I guess, because I immediately wanted to see it. I drove out here, looked around, talked to Simon for a while, and he asked if I needed a job. Seemed *he* needed a foreman, and we struck a deal. Been here ever since."

Dena leaned her back against a tree and looked off into space. Ry was here by pure chance. She'd been born to the ranch, but she was here at the present because of misfortune. And she was the only heir to the ranch because of more misfortune. She suddenly recalled overhearing a conversation—when she was still very young—with her mother saying to a lady friend that she and Simon had hoped for a large family, but she could have no more children after Dena's birth. How unfortunate, the woman friend had replied with touching sympathy.

My God, Dena thought frantically, where had that memory come from? Her mother had not been able to have more children after her birth; why, oh, why hadn't she been born a boy? Simon would have loved having a son.

There wasn't so much as a remnant of the tranquillity in her system that she'd felt only a short time ago, and, in fact, she could no longer sit there.

"Let's move on," she mumbled.

Her tone startled Ry and he sat up abruptly. "Sure thing. Whatever you say."

They each reached for the canvas bag. Their hands touched, their eyes met, and in the next instant they were kissing. There'd been no warning of a kiss, no plan to do so in either's mind, no wild chemistry driving one of them toward the other and certainly no romance in the air. And yet they kissed— softly, gently, tenderly.

It didn't last long. Each of them jumped back as though burned. Dena saw the shock she was feeling in her own soul in Ry's eyes. What in heaven's name had caused *that?* she thought, and could tell Ry was thinking the same thing.

"Uh, sorry," he mumbled, hastening to his feet.

The moment was too tense. Dena quickly rushed to alter it by giving a short, quick laugh. "Think nothing of it," she told Ry. "It was just one of those things. Didn't mean a thing."

He laughed, too, and both of them knew their laughter was as phony as a three-dollar bill. They were no longer comfortable with each other. That kiss had forever changed the tone of their relationship, and each knew it.

Mounted and riding away, neither could think of anything to say that would make the slightest sense.

Dena kept Goldie a few steps behind Ry's horse and pretended great interest in their surroundings by constantly looking around. He kept staring straight ahead, she noticed, and his back looked much stiffer than it had before they'd stopped for lunch.

She groaned silently. They'd been getting along so well. Why in heaven's name had they kissed each other? What had prompted the impulse?

And why was her silly female brain stuck on the memory

of how his lips had felt on hers? On how he smelled close up?

"Damn, damn, damn," she mouthed without sound. She couldn't put the blame on him when she'd done as much kissing as he had. Without question, it had been a mutual effort.

She groaned again.

# Seven

$R$y was truly shaken by that kiss. Dena had done nothing to cause it, and he would swear on a Bible that he hadn't been thinking of making a pass. So what had prompted it? Her laughing it off was another perturbing aspect of the incident. Naturally he'd laughed when she had. What else could he have done, gotten huffy or shown hurt feelings that she would find a kiss between them something to laugh about?

In all honesty, though, their laughter hadn't been relaxed and the sort of mirth one displayed over a good joke. Nervous laughter was a better description, and they'd both used it to get past a discomfiting situation.

Regardless, the effects of that kiss were residual. He felt differently toward Dena now and could feel a change in attitude from her. The whole thing put him on edge, and he wondered where his brain had been hiding when his hormones had suddenly leapt to life. It was a strange thing, that kiss. He'd moved closer to Dena and she'd moved closer to him, as though they had both lost all ability to think for themselves and were following instructions from some mysterious force.

He'd participated in unplanned kisses before, but none like this one. In those cases he had acknowledged physical attraction to the lady at least a *few* minutes before kissing her. Hell's bells, Dena was his employer! What kind of idiot was he?

Dena was suffering virtually the same line of thought, only hers expanded to memories of kisses she had experienced with other men, Tommy included. It was troubling to realize that no intimacy in her past had touched her in the same way as Ry's tender kiss. She could have dealt with a cocky, egotistical pass from him much easier than what had actually occurred. What was really hard to digest was how positive she was that he hadn't been thinking of a kiss any more than she, and it had happened, anyway.

She didn't want to ride with him anymore today, but neither could she tell him why. Call it cowardice or kindness, she simply could not be truthful about it. "Ry," she said as casually as she could manage, preparing herself for a believable lie. "I'm beginning to feel very stiff and sore. I think I'd better return to the compound and get off this horse."

Relief flooded Ry's system, but he spoke in the same nonchalant tone Dena had used. "Good idea. You're not used to long rides. I should have made today's excursion a short one."

Dena pulled Goldie to a stop and smiled weakly. "*I* should have known better than to plan a full day in the saddle. See you later, okay?"

Ry had also stopped his horse. "Do you want me to come by the office this evening?"

"Um, it's probably not necessary. Unless something comes up you wish to discuss, of course."

He nodded. "Okay, fine. Are you sure you can make it back all right on your own? I mean, I could ride to the compound with you, if you'd like."

"Thanks, but I'll make it just fine." She pulled Goldie's head around, aiming the mare in the direction of the ranch compound. Ry's horse began walking, also, and they angled away from each other.

Dena nudged Goldie into a trot, and the distance between the two horses rapidly increased. It wasn't really a lie she'd told Ry, Dena thought. She did feel the effects of having been on horseback since early morning. But she would have come up with an excuse to return to the compound if she'd had to manufacture one that made no sense at all. Ry would have accepted anything she'd said without questioning it. He was as glad to get away from her as she was to be riding away from him. And things had been going so well between them. What a pity, she thought with a dismal sigh.

Well, there was nothing to do but act as though it hadn't happened. She needed Ry on the ranch, certainly a lot more than he needed his job if his background was any measure. He could go out tomorrow and buy his own ranch. Maybe not one as large and impressive as the Wind River spread, but his knowledge, experience and willingness to work hard would make even a small ranch successful.

Dena winced. They had both been so awkward after that kiss, neither of them knowing where to put themselves or what to say. Why was so much happening to her? For years—other than her obsession to reconcile with her father—she had lived a quiet, organized life. Now she barely knew which end was up, and organization of any kind was almost laughable. She had to get hold of herself. She had to decide what to do with the ranch, with herself, with the future.

Tears began dribbling down her cheeks. "Oh, Daddy," she whispered in renewed anguish. "Did you think this would be easy for me, or were you hoping it wouldn't be?" She would never know what had been in Simon's mind when he'd made that trust, and that was the biggest heartache of all.

When Dena walked into the house, Nettie was waiting for her. "That woman called."

"Ellen Clark, the appraiser?"

"Yes, and she's one of the most unfriendly people I've ever talked to."

Dena frowned. "Why would she be unfriendly? What did she say?"

"She said there was absolutely no way she was going to come out here and do any appraising without you or someone else showing her around. She said, 'That's a very large ranch and I have pages of assets to inspect,'" Nettie mimicked in a snippy voice. "She said for you to call her when you could take the time from your busy schedule. Said it sarcastically, Dena. I don't mind telling you that I didn't like her attitude one little bit."

With a perplexed expression Dena laid the canvas bag on the table. "I'll call her, of course, but I don't understand why she would be sarcastic or unfriendly with you. You were only delivering my message."

"You know, after her call I started thinking about her name. Didn't one of the Hogan girls marry a Steven Clark?"

Dena's jaw dropped. "Good Lord, Ellen! I didn't put it together. Yes, Tommy's sister Ellen was married to Steve Clark." Dena took a minute to think. "Well, this won't do at all. Apparently the Hogans are still after my hide for the divorce. Dare I trust an appraisal executed by someone who so obviously dislikes me?"

Nettie sniffed disdainfully. "You'd think they'd grow up and get over it."

"At least Ellen did something with her life," Dena said with a frown of reflection. "In that family her accomplishment is worthy of admiration." Had Ellen always been working in this field and Dena simply hadn't noticed? She'd had so many problems with her marriage that keeping track of everyone in the Hogan family had been impossible. Dena tried to recall Ellen's face, but it blurred and mingled with the other Hogan women's looks. But she did remember that Ellen was one of the older kids and a good fifteen years senior to Tommy, who was the baby of the large family. Ellen was one of the Hogans she hadn't gotten to know very well, Dena recalled now. But if she had treated Nettie impolitely, then she adhered to her family's misguided belief that Dena had divorced their precious Tommy without cause.

Thoughts of the Hogans gave rise to a question. "Nettie, do you know what kind of work Tommy is doing?"

Again Nettie sniffed. "Same as always. One day a job here

and another day a job someplace else. He married again, you know.''

"No, I didn't know. You never mentioned it in any of your letters or when we talked on the phone.''

"Well, for one thing I didn't think you'd be interested, and for another it didn't last long. She was a nice girl, new to town, and I suppose taken in by Tommy's good looks. After a few months she left the area and I heard she divorced Tommy by mail.''

"Women can be such fools,'' Dena said with bitterness and a self-condemning shake of her head. "All a man has to have is a pretty face, and women fall at his feet.''

"Dena, you were only seventeen when you started dating Tommy,'' Nettie chided.

"Yes, but I knew all about his reputation. His family's, too. There's no acceptable excuse for what I did, Nettie.'' Dena's voice took on bitterness again. "And I'm still paying for it,'' she said, adding, "I'll probably pay for it the rest of my life.'' It was a painful truth that felt like a knife in her heart.

But would the pain be less acute in Seattle than it was here in her father's house, on his land?

Nettie was looking at her sadly, as though she knew exactly what Dena was thinking. Dena squared her slumped shoulders; she didn't want Nettie worrying about her. "Did Ellen leave a number where I can reach her?''

"It's on the desk in the office.''

"I'll call her now.'' Dena left the kitchen and went to the office. Seated at the desk, she stared at the phone number Nettie had written on a small piece of paper. She didn't want to make this call; she wanted nothing to do with any of the Hogans. But neither could she let them scare her off. If anything, she had to be stronger when dealing with a Hogan than she did with anyone else.

Before she could change her mind, she reached for the phone and dialed Ellen Clark's number. An answering machine switched on. "Hello, this is Ellen Clark. I'm out of the office at the present, but please leave your name and number and I'll return your call at the first available moment. Thank you.''

"Ellen, this is Dena Colby. Sorry I wasn't here when you called this morning. Call me when you can and we'll make an appointment for the appraisal. Thank you." Dena put down the phone and realized her hand wasn't steady. She sucked in a breath. This had to stop. All of it. Her indecisiveness, her misery, her constant forays into the past that did nothing but cause pain, anger and remorse. She need apologize to no one for divorcing Tommy, and there wasn't one single thing she could do about having permanently alienated her father. She had enough to deal with in the present; it was time to put the past *in* the past.

She sighed. It was easy enough to tell herself to do that, but was it possible?

All she could do was try.

That evening Dena again went to the men's dining room and asked Ry to come to the office after he ate. He nodded without a change of expression, and Dena left with her heart in her throat. That kiss might have meant nothing to him, and she'd been telling herself all afternoon that it meant nothing to her, but all she had to do was look at Ry to feel its warmth on her lips again. It should not have affected her so indelibly. It had not been a passionate kiss, after all, certainly not one that had conveyed a yearning desire on Ry's part that had simply gotten out of control. She would bet anything that Ry was wishing it hadn't happened, just as she'd been doing.

There was a stack of file folders on the desk, and Dena took the one on top and laid it open in front of her. She had started going through the file cabinet this afternoon because of her ignorance of the trust's cash position. She could have called Terry Endicott, the accountant, for the information, but she was in no mood for any more surprised reactions because she wasn't sure of what she'd inherited. One thing she was rapidly learning was that cash was a crucial component of a successful ranching operation. Not that she was sold on Ry's idea of putting in an irrigation system, but right now she couldn't do

it even if it was a dire necessity. There was too much she
didn't know.

The thing was, the transfer documents in the trust file only
cited account numbers for savings accounts and certificates of
deposit in specified banks. No sums were mentioned, just as
there were no values given to the land, the equipment and so
on. Dena could readily see why a certified appraisal was necessary for anyone to arrive at a concise, inarguable evaluation
of net worth for tax purposes. A Hogan doing the appraising
was a personally unnerving prospect, but Dena had come up
with a way for her to entirely avoid Ellen Clark, and without
insulting her, too.

In the meantime, she was getting an education from her
father's file cabinet. Thus far she had discovered numerous
bank statements with large balances and had learned that she
could afford a dozen irrigation systems and much more, and
she was still working with files from the first drawer. She'd
had no idea of the amount of cash Simon had accumulated
over the years, and the bank statements and copies of deposit
certificates—she assumed the originals were in the safety deposit box—were adding up to a startling sum.

This particular file contained correspondence between
Simon and a breeder of red Angus cattle. There were some
Angus on the ranch now, intermingled with various other
breeds. It appeared from the letters Dena began reading that
Simon had been considering specializing in Angus. In the final
letter, however, dated a month ago, he had still been unde-
cided. This was not something she wanted to spend any time
on. Dena closed the file and set it aside.

She was reaching for another when Ry walked in. Even
though she'd asked him to come to the office and had been
waiting for him, his presence jarred her. He looked freshly
shaved and showered, and was wearing clean jeans and a blue
shirt. Their eyes met, and that damned kiss lay on the path of
their gazes as heavily as a lead weight.

"Hi," he said quietly, and she dropped her eyes and drew
her hand back from the stack of folders.

"Please sit down," she said calmly, belying the ridiculously quickened beating of her heart.

Ry took the same chair he'd been using during these meetings and looked at her without saying anything, although he did wonder what had come up between their ride and this evening that required discussion. He'd sworn to behave as though that kiss hadn't taken place the next time he and Dena were together, but he hadn't expected his vow to be tested quite so soon and his impassive expression was an effort because he wasn't comfortable and suspected the same uneasiness in Dena.

She seemed to prove his suspicion by nervously clearing her throat. "There's something I'd like you to do."

"Name it." Was it a personal task to which she was referring? Some totally masculine part of his psyche hoped so, although he could conjure up no images of what it might be.

Before one single syllable came out of Dena's mouth, a picture of Ellen giving Ry an earful popped into her mind. Her stomach sank. She had been going to ask Ry to show Ellen around, but with that unnerving visual shaking Dena's very foundation, she hastily sought another solution. Ellen had not yet returned her call, and Dena could only assume that she would do so tomorrow.

"I'm expecting a call from an appraiser. She has requested that someone be available to escort her around the ranch. I'd like you to have one of the men do it."

So, he thought with a sudden acute sense of disappointment, which definitely took him by surprise, her present discomfiture had nothing to do with the two of them. He took a breath. "I'd be more than glad to do it myself, Dena," he said, thinking she would be pleased at his offer.

From her expression she wasn't at all pleased, which delivered another jab of disappointment to Ry's system. "You have enough to do keeping this place running smoothly," she said in quick response. "I have no idea how long it will take, maybe a few hours, maybe a few days, and I really would rather you assign it to one of the men." Which man? she thought frantically. Which one wouldn't listen to and encourage gossip? How could she find out? Ry was her only source of information on that score. She forged on. "I want this appraisal completed as quickly as is humanly possible. In other words, I *don't* want the man you choose for the job to dawdle his way through it. Do we have a man who will show Mrs. Clark what she wants to inspect without wasting time in idle chitchat?"

Ry thought a moment, then nodded. "Cal Fitzgerald rarely indulges in idle conversation. Can hardly get him to say two words, in fact."

"Which one is Cal?"

"He's the oldest man in the crew, sixty-three years of age. Gray hair and mustache. Been a cowhand all his life. And he knows the ranch like the back of his hand. He's worked here a long time, Dena, probably was here before you left home." He watched her closely when he said that last part, feeling shock as he realized that he would like her to open up with him, tell him what Nettie had about the Colbys' past, or rather her own version of it. What did *she* think had caused the breach between her and Simon? And what about her marriage? Had she married Tommy Hogan to spite her father, or had she really been in love?

Dena was startled and showing it. Had Cal really worked at the ranch before she'd left it? She should remember and couldn't. How...how upsetting. Her teeth clamped together in self-reproach and guilt. Had she really been so self-centered in those days that she couldn't even remember her father's hired help? Was she herself the only person who'd counted back then? My Lord, talk about a dysfunctional family, with her defiantly going her own way and Simon fumbling through attempts to deal with a rebellious daughter. And he'd always been busy with the ranch, with very little time to deal with unnecessary problems. How frustrated he must have felt.

Ry picked up a sudden tension from Dena and decided it had something to do with that appraisal. He leaned forward slightly. "Dena, my sisters and I went through probate with our parents' estate, and it's really not as bad as you might think. Takes some time, of course, but—"

Abruptly bringing herself back to the present, Dena cut in. "I don't have to go through probate."

Ry looked puzzled. "Are the probate laws that much different in Wyoming than they are in Texas?"

"I wouldn't know. The reason I'm able to avoid probate is because Dad put all of his assets into a trust. A revocable living trust," she explained further when Ry still looked perplexed.

His expression cleared some. "I've heard of that term."

Dena could tell he knew very little, if anything, about a revocable living trust. "I didn't know what it meant before John Chandler explained it, either," she said quietly. "And I'm still not all that certain that I fully understand its value. Except for avoiding probate this one time, that is."

"Well, that seems like an advantage." So, she'd inherited a trust rather than Simon's actual assets. Interesting. Did she have full control of the trust? Could she do what she wanted with it?

"Apparently it is. Anyway, the appraisal was requested by Dad's accountant for federal tax purposes."

Ry nodded. "I'll talk to Cal about showing Mrs. Clark around. Just let me know when she's coming."

"And please mention my request to hurry her through her time on the ranch as much as possible. I expect him to be tactful about it, of course."

While they talked, Ry thought about how much he was enjoying the view. Dena's looks were growing on him, and tonight he found her fresh-faced beauty and simply styled white blouse quite alluring. She had small wrists and hands, a slender creamy neck and a graceful way of moving. Her eyes were a striking gray-green color and heavily fringed with black lashes. He'd noticed her eyes before, of course, but this evening they seemed especially attractive, even while containing a harried expression.

He wanted to help her in the worst way. He'd do almost anything to help her. "Dena," he said softly, "don't let all of what's been happening get you down so much. Losing a parent is a blow, but everyone has to go through it sooner or later.

Rely on me to take care of Mrs. Clark and anything else that will ease your burden.''

She looked at him sharply. "I do not want *you* taking care of Mrs. Clark. Didn't I make myself clear enough on that point?''

Ry frowned. "I only meant that you needn't concern yourself with her. As I said before, I'll have Cal show her around. Dena—" he leaned forward "—please don't take this wrong, but you seem to jump to a conclusion awfully fast. Is that because of me? Do I ruffle your feathers or something? I know I shouldn't have kissed you today, but—"

"Don't!'' She drove the panic from her voice, and her next words sounded almost normal. "What happened at the spring was as much my fault as yours. I'd just as soon not talk about it, if you don't mind.''

He looked at her for a long moment and realized that if he was going to be honest with himself he *would* have to admit he would like to talk about it. In fact, he would like to admit it to her.

Then he'd like to ask her out. They could see a movie in Winston, or take a drive and simply talk. If she enjoyed dancing, there was a club on the edge of town with a dance floor that featured live Country bands on weekends. They could even drive to Lander and have dinner in a good restaurant. It had been a long time since he'd been truly interested in a woman, and he wished with all his heart that the woman wasn't his employer. Circumstances were not conducive to a personal relationship at the present. Maybe that would change. Time would lessen Dena's grief, and there might come a day when she would welcome an invitation for an evening out.

He would be here when that day came. Patience was one of his virtues, wasn't it?

"Whatever you say,'' he said quietly. "If you don't want to talk about it, then we won't.''

Dena couldn't quite meet his eyes. "Uh, I think that's all for tonight.''

Her tone was dismissive, and Ry got to his feet. "See you tomorrow. Good night.''

"Good night," she murmured, relieved when he walked out of the office.

Alone, she picked up a pencil, then threw it down on the desk again with a muttered oath. The last thing she needed right now was the complication of a man in her life, but there was something developing between her and Ry that she didn't seem to have any control over. To be brutally honest, if she didn't need his expertise with the ranch so badly she would ask him to leave.

But she did need him, and firing him was not one of her options. She shuddered. How could she even contemplate such a thing? She would be lost without Ry running the show.

And whatever it was that seemed to be growing between them...well, she *would* control it, dammit, she would!

Somehow.

# Eight

At seven the next morning Ellen Clark called. "Dena, I hope I didn't wake you," the woman said sweetly.

"Not at all, Ellen. I've been up since five." Dena was determined to be cordial. While married to Tommy, she'd never had a direct problem with Ellen, and she didn't know which of the Hogans had invented and spread those lies about her after the divorce. She had only been told they had come from the Hogan family. Ellen might not have had a thing to do with it. Besides, it was water under the bridge, and Dena had enough to worry about without refueling that old trouble.

"Really?" Ellen said, her tone even more saccharine. "I don't remember you as being an early riser. You do know who I am, don't you?"

"Yes, of course. And you probably don't recall my being an early riser because I was working nights as a waitress at the Winston truck stop," Dena said calmly. "Naturally I was sleeping when most folks were just getting up."

"Oh, that's right, you were, weren't you? Well, your financial situation has certainly turned around, hasn't it? No more waitressing for you, I'd bet.''

Dena sighed silently. Ellen apparently knew about her inheritance. But why wouldn't she know? Probably everyone within a fifty-mile radius of Winston knew about it, and Ellen would be more informed than most because of her assignment to appraise Simon's estate.

But she was not going to let any remark of Ellen's rile her, even one as snide as that waitressing comment. She could explain to Ellen that she'd never been ashamed of her job as a waitress, hadn't worked in that capacity in years and was now very proud of her nursing career, which she had accomplished all on her own. But she wasn't going to do that, either. Let Ellen think whatever she wanted.

"Getting down to business, Ellen, when would you like to come out to the ranch?" Dena said in a smooth-as-honey voice.

"Today," Ellen said flatly, sounding authoritative and full of herself. "I have a very tight schedule for the next ten working days, and if I don't do the appraisal today it will have to be delayed for some time."

*Perfect,* Dena thought with a slightly smug smile. Ellen had just thrown her weight around, probably hoping to put Dena on the spot, and instead had made it easy for Dena to say, "Today is fine, Ellen, although I have a pressing appointment in Lander and won't be here. One of my men will give you his full attention for as long as you need it." Dena gave a small laugh. "He knows much more about the ranch than I do, anyway."

"I doubt that," Ellen shot back sharply. "You grew up there. I'm certain you know every inch of *your* ranch." She had emphasized the word *your* so strongly that Dena's mouth dropped open. Before she could close it and say something in response, Ellen added, "Tommy said you had talked many times about the two of you living on the ranch someday. Now you have it and he doesn't. Rather unfair, wouldn't you agree?"

"Ellen!" Dena gasped in shock. "I *never* talked to Tommy

about living on the ranch. That was the furthest thing from my mind in those days. If he said that, he lied.''

"You're calling my brother a liar? *I* think it's the other way around, Dena."

This conversation was evolving into a cat fight. Dena took a breath and gritted her teeth. She was *not* going to be drawn into all-out war with Ellen or any other Hogan.

"Ellen, let's keep this impersonal. What's past is past and neither of us can change it. What time should I tell my man to expect you?"

After several seconds of heavy silence, Ellen said sullenly, "I'll be there around nine."

"The name of your escort for however long you need him is Cal Fitzgerald. He'll be waiting for you. Goodbye, Ellen." Dena put down the phone. Her hands clenched into fists.

Her first thought was to immediately call Terry Endicott and tell him that she did not want Ellen doing the appraisal. She couldn't possibly be the only certified appraiser in the area. In the next instant Dena realized how tightly her fists were clenched, and she forced her hands to relax. She had allowed Ellen get to her on a personal level, and if she asked Terry to dismiss Ellen and hire another appraiser, the Hogans would undoubtedly raise some kind of hell from now to kingdom come.

She would not give them that satisfaction. They were the sort of people who thrived on dissension and gossip, and would probably be thrilled to have another reason to run down her character. Besides, if Ellen's appraisal came in at some ridiculous figure, Terry would know.

*I'm just not going to worry about it,* Dena told herself as she got up from the desk. One thing required no debate at all; she was not going to be here when Ellen arrived. Hurrying through the house, she went outside to find Ry. When she didn't immediately spot him in the compound, she became nervous. What if he'd taken a horse and gone to a far corner of the ranch? He didn't just hang around the compound, after all. He was a worker himself and head man of the crew. He could be anywhere.

Dena peered into several buildings, getting more alarmed by the minute. They needed some sort of communication system, whereby everyone on the ranch could stay in touch with each other. Those hand-held radios that police officers used, for example, would work beautifully for a large ranch.

She felt enormous relief when she entered the largest barn and saw Ry at the far end, just coming out of a stall. "Ry?" she called.

He saw her coming toward him and began walking to meet her halfway. The back of his neck prickled and a frisson of sexual energy traveled his spine. He wasn't a man to kid himself, and he knew in that instant that he wanted Dena Colby. It hadn't been instantaneous attraction between them; to the contrary, what he felt now had snuck up on him when he wasn't looking. It was the same overwhelming force that had caused that unexpected kiss, he thought with a grimness caused by the knowledge that he didn't like the idea of falling for his boss and it was happening, anyway.

"Morning," he said, speaking curtly so Dena couldn't possibly garner a hint of where his thoughts had been.

She frowned slightly because he sounded almost angry, but she had no time to delve into any problem he might be having to deal with this morning. "Ry, Ellen Clark, the appraiser I told you about, just called. She'll be here around nine this morning. Can you have Cal prepared for her arrival by then?"

Ry nodded. "Don't see why not."

Dena breathed a relieved sigh. "Great. I won't be here, so it's entirely in your hands. As I said last night, tell Cal to give Mrs. Clark his full attention and to take her anywhere on the ranch she wants to go." *Funny how one's mind works,* she was thinking while she talked. She had lied to Ellen about a "pressing" appointment in Lander, but she did not want to tell the same lie to Ry. Actually she hadn't liked lying to Ellen, either; it had just seemed a prudent move. Besides, the Hogans already thought she was a liar and worse, when she wasn't, for heaven's sake, and they didn't deserve her respect. Ry did.

"I'm driving to Lander. Is there anything you need for the

ranch? I could pick it up while I'm there,'' she said, intentionally avoiding the word *appointment*.

"Nothing I can think of off the top of my head," Ry replied. He expected her to turn and go, but she remained where she was.

"Ry, I was thinking of something a few minutes ago. You know those little two-way radios—I think they used to call them walkie-talkies—but anyway the police use them, or something like them. Anyhow, I was thinking how useful it would be to have some sort of communication system so the men could stay in touch with each other. What do you think about it?''

"I think it's a great idea."

"I wonder what they would cost."

"Probably two, three hundred dollars a unit."

Dena frowned. ''That much?''

"Could be more. I've never priced two-way radios, so I'm only guessing at cost." Ry was watching her closely. Her coming up with *any* idea to improve the efficiency of the ranch's operation was a major change in attitude. "To be completely effective they would have to be high-powered units, Dena. There'd be no point in buying anything with only a short-range coverage.''

"That's true," she murmured thoughtfully. "Well, maybe I'll look into it. I'd better go now. I'll probably be gone all day, so I'll see you this evening.''

Ry walked her to the barn door. The sunlight brought life to her hair, highlighting its rich, dark color. She was wearing jeans, brown loafers and a red blouse, and she was suddenly the prettiest little woman he'd ever seen.

Dena tilted her head to look up at his face. Why, there were strands of gray in the dark hair around his ears, she thought, startled that she hadn't noticed that before. And some lines in his face. He had to be ten years older than her twenty-five years, maybe more, but his maturity was incredibly becoming. She flushed when she realized they had been looking at each other for several seconds, and that his navy blue eyes contained a hot light of intense admiration.

"Well," she said breathlessly.

"Yes, well," Ry said with a little half smile. He felt especially good. That long look between them meant something, and the only explanation he could come up with was that Dena was as attracted to him as he was to her. Maybe falling for the boss was okay, after all.

"Gotta get going," Dena mumbled, walking off with her cheeks burning.

Ry's smile became fully developed. He stood there with a lovely warm feeling in his chest and watched her hurrying to the house, and he didn't move until she was inside with the door closed. Life had just become a hundred times more exciting, and he hadn't even been looking for excitement; it had happened all on its own. Fate, apparently.

Whistling, he left the front door of the barn to hike to the far corral where he had Cal working with a young, unbroken horse. The older man was especially talented with horses, as patient as any handler Ry had ever seen, and he liked Cal's gentle way of training a yearling to the saddle.

Ry leaned on the corral fence. "Got a minute, Cal?" The older man left the colt and came to the fence without a word. "I have a special job for you today," Ry said.

Cal nodded. "Okay."

"A certified appraiser, a woman by the name of Ellen Clark, is coming to appraise the ranch. It has something to do with estate taxes. Anyway, she needs an escort for the day or however long it takes her to do the job. I'd like you to handle it."

"Ellen Clark, you say? Dena's former sister-in-law?"

For a second Ry was stumped for an answer. Then his eyes narrowed. *That* was why Dena couldn't leave fast enough. And also the reason she'd refused Ry's offer to deal with the appraiser himself, and had asked for a man who wouldn't dawdle the time away in idle chitchat. *Chitchat, my eye. What is it that Dena's afraid of where Ellen Clark is concerned? Something from her past that Nettie had omitted from her story and Mrs. Clark would be only too happy to pass on to anyone who would listen?*

"Guess so," Ry said casually. "Do you mind showing her around?"

Cal looked longingly back at the young horse. "Ry, I'd rather walk on hot coals, but you're the boss."

Ry couldn't help laughing. "Thanks, Cal. She'll be here around nine."

During the drive to Lander, Dena talked herself out of investigating the cost of two-way radios. She wasn't going to spend her father's money on anything unnecessary, even though she was beginning to believe there was a great deal of cash in the estate. But it didn't feel like *her* cash, and maybe it never would. She really didn't like thinking about it and decided to find something to do in Lander that would take her mind completely off the ranch.

In the next heartbeat, however, she *was* thinking about the ranch, or rather, its foreman. Ry Hardin was like no other man she'd ever known, and she was beginning to feel very soft and womanly when she was with him. Could he tell? She could tell he liked her, so why wouldn't he sense similar feelings from her?

But what, really, made him different? *Why* was she getting a little weak in the knees around him? Was it his maturity? His craggy face? His size? Dena sighed. She liked his looks and she might as well admit it, but she'd met other handsome men since her divorce and they hadn't affected her an iota. What she liked about Ry was his maturity, she decided, his self-assurance. He seemed to be a man who knew exactly what he wanted out of life and was getting it. He had an air of stability, of rock-hard steadfastness, and at the same time, possessed a kindly nature.

A little bell went off in her head. Ry was also the man she'd overheard saying that he would never marry again. Given Ry's resolute personality, it would be a foolish mistake to think he went around saying things he didn't mean.

But she wasn't looking for a husband, for pity's sake! Why had she put Ry and the idea of marriage in the same thought? "Idiot," she mumbled, her eyes on the road. She was as leery of a second marriage as Ry was. Of course there were other relationships for a man and woman, although except for very casual friendships with men she hadn't done any experimenting.

Maybe she had become a little *too* independent, Dena mused. Her divorce had forced independence upon her, and it had accelerated from there. It was satisfying to know she could support herself and be contented with a simple life-style, but, looking back, she'd also had her share of lonely moments.

Was she lonely now? The ranch wasn't the same without her father; was that the reason she was gradually turning to Ry?

Dena sighed again, this time with exasperation. Was there anything less productive than soul-searching? Maybe there were answers within herself, maybe not, but would she even recognize one if it suddenly leapt to life in her brain? She wasn't happy in Wyoming and she wouldn't be happy in Seattle now, either. She'd lost too much of herself when she lost her father. It wasn't fair that he'd died so young and left her feeling as empty as a cistern after a three-year draught. Empty, sick at heart, and knowing there was no way she could ever correct the mistakes she'd made that had severed their relationship.

Wiping away a tear, she told herself to stop being so damned gloomy. It was a pretty, sunshiny day, and she'd told Nettie not to expect her until this evening. Surely she could find something to do in Lander to cheer herself up.

Whether she managed to do that or not, she was going to give it her best shot.

Ry opened the driver's door of the bright red four-wheel Bronco that had just arrived. "Mrs. Clark?"

The woman behind the wheel smiled at him. She looked to be around forty, was dressed nicely in tan slacks and a striped blouse, and all in all struck Ry as an attractive lady.

"Cal Fitzgerald?" Ellen said while getting out of her vehicle.

"No, Cal's over there by the fence. I'm Ry Hardin, ranch

foreman. Since I was nearby when I saw you driving in, I thought I'd say hello." He honestly hadn't planned to do this, but when he'd spotted the red Bronco, curiosity had suddenly gotten the best of him.

Ellen held out her hand, which Ry shook. "Good meeting you, Mr. Hardin."

"Good meeting you, Mrs. Clark. Are you all set for the tour?"

Turning back to the Bronco, she reached inside for a clipboard containing a half-inch sheaf of papers and a large bag that Ry figured doubled for a briefcase and purse. She closed the vehicle's door. "I'd like to inspect the buildings before I look at the land, Mr. Hardin."

"We'll do it in any order you wish, ma'am." Ry beckoned to Cal, who began a lackadaisical stroll toward them.

"That includes the house, of course," Ellen said. "In fact, I believe I'll start with the house."

Cal walked up. Ry introduced him, and the older man mumbled, "Pleased to meetcha."

An inquisitive expression entered Ellen's eyes. "Have we met before, Mr. Fitzgerald? You seem familiar."

"Been around these parts a long time," Cal muttered. "I know who you are, so maybe you've seen me a few times. But, nope, we ain't never met."

"Hmm," Ellen said, appearing to be thinking that over. Then she became businesslike. "I won't need you for about a half hour, Mr. Fitzgerald. I'm going to inspect the house first." Her gaze moved back to Ry. "I know Dena's not here, but is anyone in the house?"

"Nettie Bascomb," Ry replied.

"Oh, yes, Nettie. Well, I'll go and get started. See you later."

Ry and Cal watched her stride quickly to the back door of the house. "Seems nice enough," Ry murmured. Cal snorted. Ry raised an eyebrow, but Cal was already walking off. "Where will you be?" Ry called.

"At the corral," Cal said over his shoulder, sounding disgusted.

Ry grinned and shook his head. Cal could be as cantankerous as a bear with a thorn in its paw. Obviously he wanted Ry to get the message—again—that he wasn't thrilled with this assignment. For a few moments Ry toyed with the idea of disregarding Dena's instructions and dealing with Ellen Clark himself. His curiosity about the woman and her role in Dena's past had not been even slightly appeased by a hello and a handshake.

But *why* was he curious? He already knew all about Dena's short-term marriage and the trouble it had caused with Simon, didn't he? What else could there be besides the story Nettie had told him? So Ellen Clark had been Dena's sister-in-law. Would he discuss Dena with her or anyone else even if they were foaming at the mouth with eagerness to tell old tales?

No, he didn't want to hear any more secondhand stories about the Colbys, he decided. Since when had he become interested in gossip, anyway? Striding to the main corral for his horse, he saddled the animal, mounted and rode to the training corral. "Cal," he called. "I'm going to be busy. Keep an eye on the house and watch for Mrs. Clark. See you later." He rode away.

It was early evening when Dena left Lander and started the drive home. There was a relaxed sensation in her system that she hadn't felt since Ry's grievous phone call to Seattle; apparently a day away from the ranch and its accompanying problems had done some good. What she'd found to do to use up a whole day was shopping, and she was sure she had visited every store in Lander that carried women's clothing and accessories. The back seat of her car was loaded with packages containing new things for herself. There was also a gift for Nettie. Dena hadn't brought nearly enough clothing with her from Seattle, and she'd been getting very tired of wearing the same things again and again.

But there was no question that she had purchased prettier, more brightly colored, more expensive things than she was accustomed to wearing. She'd used her own credit cards and had run up some high balances, which didn't start bothering her until she was about halfway home. She had never spent

so much money on clothes at one time in her life, so did this
shopping spree indicate an acceptance of her inheritance? Was
she finally admitting that she was happy about inheriting the
ranch? Thankful that her father had included her in the trust?

It was getting dark, and the Wyoming countryside bore a
silvery, twilight sheen. There was a quietude here that no city
could attain, not even in its outer areas. Wyoming's rural roads
saw very little traffic. Ranch compounds were few and far
between. Animals wandered on open range, and it was as normal to spot a herd of antelope as it was a herd of cattle. A
sentimental clog in her throat took Dena by surprise. Wyoming
was home and she loved it. Now that she was back, could she
possibly leave again?

*But there is so much heartache connected to staying,* a voice
in her head argued. *Could you live with that? With the memories that would never leave you be? You haven't even mustered the courage to step foot in your father's bedroom, how
would you get past the memories?*

"My memories of home aren't all bad," she whispered in
debate with the voice. Those of the years before her mother
became ill warmed her heart. That was when the Colbys had
been a true family. A loving family. There'd been picnics,
horseback rides together and laughter. Simon had always been
more serious than jovial, but Dena couldn't doubt that he'd
loved her as a child. Then that awful disease had struck Opal,
and her illness had been like an impenetrable cloud shrouding
the sun. Everyone had tried to keep smiling and act as though
life was normal. It wasn't, and there was no more laughter.

Dena's mind flitted, recalling bits and pieces of her teenage
years. Had Simon ever really laughed again after his wife's
death? Had she, other than with her school friends? She remembered hating to go home after school on some days, and
of spending hours on horseback once she got there. Riding by
herself until darkness forced her back to the compound. Simon
began taking the evening meal with the men, and Dena ate
with Nettie. Father and daughter had grown farther and farther
apart.

Dena sighed from the sadness of it all, and because it had

been so terribly unnecessary. If only she'd had the maturity to understand the depth of her father's grief, or if he had been able to talk about his pain with her. Their tragic loss had been mutual and should have brought them closer together instead of tearing them apart.

Dena switched on the headlights with another sigh. Why did she keep going over it again and again? Was it a form of self-punishment because she had caused the final breach with her father?

She suddenly felt very alone on this remote Wyoming road and became anxious to get back to the ranch. Nettie was there…and Ry.

Her heart skipped a beat as she pictured Ry in her mind's eye. He was handsome, strong and steady, and a man who could be described as a truly nice guy. She had become very dependent on Ry, which was unusual when she'd been almost fanatically independent for years now. But inside of her there were more feelings than that sense of needing Ry because of the ranch. Did *she* need him? Did she want him, as a woman wanted a man?

A fluttering nervousness began tweaking the pit of her stomach. Putting Ry and romance in the same thought was disturbing. But she would like to get to the bottom of this discomfiting conjecture—was it romance she was thinking about…or sex?

A thrilling excitement suddenly coursed through her body. It followed her veins and sensitized her nerve endings. It traveled her spine and prickled the hairs on the back of her neck. It caused a rise in temperature, with a particularly warm, achy spot at the juncture of her thighs. To say the bombardment of her senses was startling would be an understatement of enormous proportions; she had never, *never* undergone such an astounding reaction to the mere thought of sex.

Rolling down her window, she breathed deeply of the cool night air flowing into the car. It helped, though it didn't entirely return her system to normal. Would anything? she wondered with a concerned furrow between her eyes. Other than putting Ry completely out of her mind, which she didn't seem able to do.

Good Lord, how would she face the man with these ridiculous cravings running rampant within her? Wouldn't he know something was different about her just from looking into her eyes?

Her next thought was another surprise: Would Ry like how she looked in her pretty new clothes? Her frown deepened. It seemed she had little control over her thoughts and feelings where Ry was concerned. How strange, and what if he thought she'd bought new things to appear more attractive to him?

*Maybe you did.* "But I didn't," she exclaimed out loud. "I simply needed more clothes than I brought with me." *Yes, but why didn't you just buy some more jeans and plain tops?*

Well, she thought with a huge gulp of the cool air coming in the window, she had certainly given herself another problem to deal with, hadn't she? What did she want from Ry, an affair? Dare she forget his philosophy on commitment? On a second marriage? She already had enough to cope with; did she need that sort of relationship to worry about along with everything else?

"You darned fool," she muttered under her breath. "Stay away from Ry. You haven't got the sense God gave a goose." Ry had kissed her, yes, and being a man he would probably take her to bed with just the slightest provocation. But then what?

She turned into the ranch driveway on automatic pilot, drove the distance and parked next to the house. After switching off the ignition she sat there for a few moments. Her imagination had run wild during the last ten miles, she told herself. That was all that had happened. She certainly was not going to flirt or act silly around Ry. Most definitely she was not going to knowingly start something with him that might end badly, like his leaving the ranch, for instance. What on earth would she do without him running the place?

And she had *not* bought those pretty skirts, blouses, dresses, lingerie, shoes and slacks for Ry's benefit. She'd merely needed something to perk up her own spirits.

With that thought fixed firmly in her mind, she got out of the car and began to unload the back seat.

# Nine

Nettie met Dena at the back door. The older woman's eyes widened when she saw the armload of packages Dena was carrying. "Goodness, what have you there?"

"I did some shopping," Dena said. "I have more in the car, so I'll take these on to my bedroom. Be right back." She hurried to her room, deposited the parcels on her bed and returned to the kitchen. Nettie smiled, displaying pleasure that Dena had used the day to do something as normal as shopping. It was a good sign, Nettie felt, a sign of healing.

Dena smiled, too, then went outside to get the rest of her purchases. She was back in minutes. This armload was placed on the table. "I have something for you," she told Nettie.

Nettie's face lit up. "For me?"

Dena was digging through the sacks on the table. "Yes. I saw this and thought of you. I hope you like it." She handed Nettie a package, which the housekeeper promptly opened to reveal a carefully folded, pale aqua garment.

Nettie shook it out and exclaimed, "It's a dress! Oh, Dena,

it's beautiful.'' She examined the size tag. ''How did you remember my size after all these years?''

Dena smiled and shrugged. ''You like it, then?''

''I most certainly do like it. It's just beautiful.'' Laying the dress on top of the sacks and packages on the table, Nettie put her arms around Dena and gave her a hug. ''Thank you, honey. You always were a thoughtful girl.''

Dena returned Nettie's hug, then stepped back with a downcast expression. ''That's a kind sentiment, Nettie, but we both know it's not true. I wasn't thoughtful with Dad.''

''Dena, you have to stop beating yourself up over the past,'' Nettie said quietly while picking up her new dress and fingering the soft fabric. ''You were barely more than a child when all that happened, and you tried as hard as anyone could to make amends. I know you've been unhappy, and grief is perfectly natural when a person loses a loved one. But don't carry it too far, honey. You're hurting yourself unnecessarily, and I really don't think your father would have approved.''

Nettie's concern brought tears to Dena's eyes. ''I know,'' she said softly. But it wasn't true. She didn't know what Simon would have approved of, other than walking a very straight, narrow, regimented and virtuous path. It was how he had lived himself, and what he had expected from her. She simply hadn't measured up, she thought with a sad sigh. As for ''hurting herself unnecessarily,'' could she ever hurt herself as much as Simon had? That hurting business went both ways; they had hurt each other. Only, Simon had not had a forgiving nature.

''Put your new things away,'' Nettie said, speaking sympathetically. ''Did you have supper in Lander?''

Dena gathered her wits about her, drawing away from the past to concentrate on the present. ''Yes, I ate around five.'' She began picking up her packages.

''Would you like me to fix you something? A sandwich, maybe?''

''No, Nettie, thanks. I'm not a bit hungry. Oh, did you see anything of Ellen Clark while she was here?''

Nettie's lips pursed. ''Indeed I did. She and her tape measure were all over the house, and some of her comments about it weren't exactly flattering. She's an extremely annoying woman, isn't she?"

"What did she say about the house?"

"Well, for one thing she said it's old-fashioned."

Dena smiled. "It is, Nettie."

"Well, it wasn't her place to say so."

"Probably not, but she wasn't wrong, all the same. I'm going to put away these things." Dena left with her bundles. At least she had made one wise move since her homecoming, she thought on the way to her bedroom: she had avoided Ellen Hogan Clark today. Nettie was in a snit over Ellen's tactless remarks, but she'd get over it. At least Dena didn't have something to regret this evening, such as having dealt with Ellen herself and losing her temper at some point in the day. And that possibility wasn't all that difficult to imagine, either. Dena hadn't realized it before returning to Wyoming, but she harbored a grudge for the Hogan family. Maybe it was petty of her, and certainly it wasn't something of which she was proud, but they were such exasperating people. Truth was, once she'd gotten to know Tommy's family she had realized that he'd been the best of the lot. That revelation had occurred *after* she'd come to understand her husband's apathetic attitude toward a steady job, let alone any kind of career, which had made it even more startling.

Oh, well, Dena thought with a sigh of finality. She'd had her day with the Hogans and didn't plan a rematch. If she was lucky, Ellen's visit to the ranch today would be her final contact with a Hogan. Of course there was always the chance of running into one of them on the streets of Winston. Should that nauseating event ever occur, Dena vowed to hold her tongue.

Her new clothes were hanging in the closet when Dena heard a light rapping on her door. "Yes?" she called as she walked to the door to open it. It was Nettie, wearing her new dress and beaming from ear to ear.

"I tried it on for you to see. What do you think?" Nettie said.

"It's wonderful. You look beautiful in it. I was sure you would."

"Well, I just love it. I'm going to save it for a special occasion. It would be perfect for a wedding, don't you think?"

"Perfect for any semiformal affair," Dena agreed, ignoring Nettie's not-so-subtle hint that it was time Dena remarried. Nettie had stated in various letters over the years that she hoped Dena had found a nice man to date and fall in love with. In her own letters to Nettie, Dena's response had been: "I haven't met anyone important, Nettie. Maybe it will happen someday, maybe not, but I'm not at all concerned about my single status. Please don't worry about me in that regard."

"I'll take it off now." Nettie started to go, then stopped. "I almost forgot. After supper Ry came to the kitchen and asked if I knew when you'd be back. He didn't do any explaining, but I think he needs to talk to you about something."

Dena's heart skipped a beat. She hadn't planned on seeing Ry tonight, and the prospect was unnerving. Besides, he stayed in the men's bunkhouse and she wasn't at all pleased with the idea of knocking on that door after dark. The bunkhouse was the only building on the ranch that had been off limits to her while growing up. *It's the men's home while they're working here,* her father had told her sternly. *And it's no place for a young girl to be hanging around. Stay away from it.* It was one order Dena had never questioned.

"There's a phone in the bunkhouse now," Nettie said.

Dena's eyes widened. "There is? When did that happen?"

"After Ry started working here. I'm pretty sure it was his idea, because your dad never spent money on luxuries, as you well know. I overheard the tail end of a conversation between Ry and Simon one time, and Simon was frowning over the cost of bringing in a second phone line. Seemed pretty reluctant to my eyes and ears, but apparently Ry talked him into it, and, you know, after that phone was installed, Simon loved it. Especially when it was forty below outside and he needed to discuss something with Ry or one of the other men. Oh, the number is 555-3300."

Dena was visibly relieved. "Thanks, Nettie. I'll call the bunkhouse and find out what Ry wanted to see me about."

"Well, I'm going to say good-night, honey. Thanks again for this lovely dress."

"You're very welcome, Nettie. Good night and sleep well."

Dena followed Nettie into the hall. Nettie went into her bedroom and Dena continued on to the office. She sat at the desk, reached for the phone then drew her hand back. She was nervous about calling Ry and knew why, too. She'd had such brazen, intimate thoughts about Ry and herself today that she was afraid of talking to him. What if he heard something in her voice that gave her away? Wouldn't she just die of embarrassment if he caught on that she had mentally measured every inch of his ruggedly masculine body?

Getting up, Dena walked around the desk, through the office door and wandered into the kitchen. Nettie had extinguished the ceiling light, so the room was only dimly lit with reflected light from the hall. Dena went to the window over the sink and peered outside. The bunkhouse was visible from here, and she could see several lit-up windows. Some of the men might have retired for the night, but not all of them.

Not Ry, she thought with intuitive conviction. Maybe it *was* important that he speak to her tonight, although she couldn't imagine what could be so urgent.

Unless it had something to do with Ellen's visit today.

Dena's heart sank, but at the same time she felt a sprouting anger. If Ellen had dared to repeat those old lies about her to Cal... A much worse scenario stopped Dena cold. What if Ellen had cornered Ry? Was she unscrupulous enough to attempt to undermine Dena's authority on the ranch by filling her foreman's mind with garbage? Dena's uneasy contemplation took her further. What if Ry believed those lies and decided he didn't want to work for a woman of dubious character?

Standing there in the kitchen tense as a coiled spring, Dena asked herself if she *wanted* to know what had taken place today during her absence. Especially, did she want to know about it tonight, so she could take it to bed with her and then roll and toss till dawn?

Turning abruptly, she started from the kitchen. Whatever Ry wanted to talk to her about was going to have to wait until morning; she was going to bed.

She was just stepping into the hall beyond the kitchen doorway when a quiet knock came from the back door. Dena immediately knew who was out there: Ry.

"Oh, damn," she whispered. If she didn't answer the door would he go away? But what if he'd seen her at the window? She couldn't compound whatever sins had taken place today with rudeness.

Reluctantly, and all but dragging her feet, she made her way to the back door and opened it. Even though she *knew* who was on the back porch, facing Ry eye to eye—even in dim lighting—was a shock she hadn't expected. Today's stupid, juvenile fantasies had caused irreparable damage; she could not look at Ry without thinking of them, and she wished suddenly that she were anywhere but where she was.

"I saw you drive in a while ago," Ry said. "Thought Nettie would tell you to phone the bunkhouse, but guess she forgot." Why did she seem to be on the verge of bolting? He frowned. "Is anything wrong?"

*Yes! I think I'm falling in love with you.* Her face flushed crimson, and she thanked God that she hadn't turned on the ceiling light before answering the door. They could see each other well enough because of the yard lights and the diffused lighting coming into the kitchen from the hall, but details, such as a blush from hell, were not clearly defined.

Cold night air was seeping into the house. She couldn't keep him standing on the porch with the door open. She took a step back. "Come in."

"Thanks."

"We'll talk in the office." Dena led the way, recalling that the lights were on in the office and hoping to high heaven that her childish blush would be gone when they got there.

She stopped and let Ry enter the room before her, then closed the door. "Nettie went to bed," she said by way of explanation. "I'd rather not disturb her." Walking around the desk she sat down.

Ry sat too. "Did you have a good day in Lander?"

His question, which Dena read as rather personal, took her by surprise. "Um, yes, I...I suppose I did," she stammered. She wanted to know what had taken place with Ellen today, and yet she didn't—a quandary that made her feel on edge and uncomfortable.

Still, they couldn't just sit there and stare at each other. In fact, she wished Ry would *stop* staring at her. The power of his eyes could turn anyone into a gibbering idiot, she thought in defense of the anxious knot in her stomach. What if she really was falling in love with him? Certainly she could feel his magnetism clear across the desk as though it were something tangible. How did a woman appear dignified and composed around a man who caused such potent reactions within her? And how had this inner confusion come to be? When she'd first met Ry she had barely noticed he was male; now it was almost all she thought of. If that wasn't asking for more trouble than she deserved, what was?

"I thought you'd want to know how today went," Ry said with a curious, speculative gleam in his eye. He'd seen Dena in many different moods, most of them morose, but he couldn't quite get a handle on what she was thinking tonight.

Dena's body stiffened with dread, yet she couldn't reveal her private fears about Ellen and old lies to Ry. "I expect it went as...expected." She had wanted to speak confidently and mentally winced at how lame she sounded. She cleared her throat and tried again. "I'm sure everything went well. There's no reason why it shouldn't have. Cal did his job, didn't he? What could have gone wrong?"

"Nothing went wrong that I know of," Ry said slowly, wondering why he was suddenly picking up panic from her. "But that's what I thought you'd be glad to hear."

"And the *only* reason you're here?" Sounded like a mighty weak pretext for a meeting to her. Her cheeks got pink again. Goodness, he hadn't used *that* as an excuse to see her tonight, had he? The idea flustered her, and she spoke much too rapidly, one word stumbling over the next. "I *am* glad everything went well. Thank you for telling me."

Ry began to understand what was going on with Dena. She'd seen through his feeble motive for this meeting and it unnerved her. What was thrilling was that if she hadn't liked him as a man she wouldn't be discombobulated, she'd be angry or, at the very least, annoyed.

He sat back in his chair, pleased with his diagnosis of the situation. Still, here they were, attracted to each other and neither of them doing one damned thing about it. They weren't kids—why were they pussyfooting around each other? He wasn't afraid of her, but was she afraid of him? Maybe it was time to get a few things out in the open.

"You know I didn't come over here just to tell you everything's all right, don't you?" he said softly. "Nettie's in bed and so are the men. Why are you still up? Why am I?"

Dena squirmed in her chair. "Are you trying to put me on some sort of spot?" Ry's eyes took on a sensuous cast, which made Dena squirm again. Because the desk was so large there was at least five feet of space between them, and yet she felt crowded, as though he was standing over her.

"Is that what it feels like to you?" Ry asked. "Sorry about that. Putting you on the spot is not now nor ever was my intention." He paused briefly. "But I do think we should talk. Dena, do you know what I see when I look at you?"

All of her fantasizing today hadn't prepared her for this. How could he introduce such a personal topic in such impersonal surroundings? And out of the blue, to boot? This was a conversation that should take place in some dimly lit café or lounge, or maybe in a car parked in a private little nook somewhere, with a full moon overhead and soft, romantic music on the radio, not in this drab office with that massive desk between them.

Nervously she cleared her throat. "Ry, have I led you to believe...uh, what I mean is, have I...led you on?" She couldn't look at him.

"I don't think either of us has been doing any leading—

not consciously—other than that kiss, which in my opinion took us both by surprise. Am I wrong?''

"No, which makes your question all the more...uh, startling." She was still looking everywhere but into his eyes.

"So, what's happening between us is startling to you. Dena, it's just as startling for me. Guess you wouldn't know that, though, since we've both been acting like that kiss never took place. You didn't answer my question...are you going to?"

Dena took a breath. "I'm sure you see the same thing I do when I look into a mirror."

"Which is?"

"Are you asking me to describe myself?"

"From your point of view, yes."

She gave a short, sharp laugh. "That's silly, Ry."

He grinned, looking boyish to Dena's eyes. "Maybe it is, but you know something? I *feel* a little silly around you. Silly in a nice way. Silly in a way I haven't felt in a good many years. I think that's what I wanted you to know." He fell silent for a long moment—the grin had vanished—then said quietly, "I want to kiss you right now more than I've ever wanted anything."

Her gaze flew to his face, and she couldn't look away again. The emotion in his eyes wasn't pretense, she realized. Her heart started pounding. She watched him get up from his chair and slowly move around the desk. She heard him say, "You're so beautiful, Dena, so head-to-toe perfect." She felt him turn her chair, take her hands and pull her to her feet.

"I—I'm not," she whispered hoarsely.

"Ah, but you are. That's what I was getting at before. I see you as an unusually beautiful woman, and I was hoping you felt beautiful." His voice got deeper and huskier. "How could you not?" Gently he pulled her forward until there was no more than an inch of empty space between their bodies. His eyes were hot and caressing, and she felt their impact race through her system. She moistened her lips with the tip of her tongue and breathed in tiny, muffled gasps. She knew he was going to kiss her, and she was certain there was permission and invitation and acquiescence in *her* eyes because it was how she felt inside. And soft, oh, so soft and female. All liquidy and without an ounce of real strength.

He let go of her hands and very slowly moved his up her arms to her shoulders, then to her throat and finally to each side of her face. The hair on the back of her neck prickled, her spine tingled, and a fiery blossoming began tormenting the pit of her stomach.

She parted her lips, let her eyelids droop and watched his face coming closer to hers as he lowered his head. A second before his mouth reached hers she saw him close his eyes. Sighing ecstatically, she shut her own.

This kiss wasn't even a second cousin to the one they'd exchanged near the spring. This kiss tantalized and teased and had Dena straining against Ry's hard body in moments, all the time it took their embrace to evolve from tender to passionate. His hands left her face to slide around her body and bring her even closer, and she made little snuggling movements to *get* closer. She knew in that precise instant that she was his if he wanted her. And if his wet, hot kisses were any indication, he wanted her desperately.

*Desperation* was the perfect word to describe the tenor of their kisses and caresses, Dena thought somewhere in the hodgepodge of her befuddled mind. She wanted to undress for Ry, and to undress him. She wanted to lie on her back and have him on top of her. But where could this happen? Not in the house with Nettie in it, and Ry slept in a bunkhouse with four other men.

Ry was having no such inhibiting thoughts. Crooking an elbow around her neck, he kissed her mouth and unbuttoned her blouse with his free hand. "Dena, sweetheart," he whispered raggedly between that kiss and the next. His hand went into her blouse, found the clasp of her bra and flipped it apart. Pushing her bra aside was a simple matter after that, and the sensation of holding and touching her bare breasts—ripe and full, they were—almost undid him.

Dena moaned when he dipped his head and took a nipple into his mouth. His tongue toyed with it while he gently suckled, and her knees just kept getting weaker until she marveled that they were able to support her. The next shock to her system was his hand inside her jeans and panties.

"Ry..." She tore her mouth from his and, breathing so hard she could barely speak, managed to rasp, "We can't. Not in here."

He blinked, as though coming awake. "Doesn't the door have a lock?"

"No," she whispered, gazing longingly into his desire-glazed eyes. "Nettie..." She let the implication dangle.

To her surprise he began buttoning her blouse. "I know where we can go," he told her.

"Where?"

"You'll see."

She took his hands and spoke breathlessly. "Wait...I...I'm not sure."

His eyes, hot and heavy, bored into her. "You were sure a minute ago."

The desire in the air was almost palpable. They were each breathing irregularly. He wanted her, and she couldn't deny that she felt the same yearning for him.

"Where...where were you taking me?" she whispered unsteadily.

"To the loft of the barn. You have to remember the odds and ends of old furniture stored up there. Sometimes when the men are playing cards and I need my own space, I go to the loft to sleep. There's a bed—nothing fancy—but the bedding is clean, and it's comfortable enough. No one else ever goes up there. It's quiet...and private."

"Oh." She *did* remember the loft being used for storage. She had played up there as a child, using the clutter to suit her girlish fantasies and games. Sometimes the place was a castle and she was a princess. Sometimes she was a storekeeper and everything was for sale. Imaginary customers would appear in her mind, and she would hold long conversations with them. *This bureau was brought from the East on a prairie schooner in 1880. As you can see it's made of excellent wood and only needs a bit of furniture polish.* The bureau in question, Dena recalled, had been an ancient old thing, scarred and pocked, with drawers without handles and a broken leg. As a youngster she had definitely possessed a vivid imagination.

What had happened to that wonderful trait? She knew it was long gone and that she looked at everything from a totally realistic point of view. Even her sense of humor was muted around most people. A shocking thought struck her: She was becoming more like her father every day!

Looking into Ry's feverish eyes, she lifted her chin. She would *not* become old before her time, as Simon had, and if she ever had children she would never, never shut them out, not for any reason. She would not destroy their imaginations with too much sternness, and she would encourage their laughter and personal strengths, especially when faced with serious events.

Ry could tell she was thinking, possibly weighing what was happening between them against ingrained rules of behavior. He wanted her to know this was not a passing fancy with him, but he wasn't sure just how it should be said.

He moved his hands so they were clasping hers. "Dena, I would never try to talk you into something that felt morally wrong to you. Is that what's bothering you?"

The breath she drew was shaky, but she squared her shoulders. "I guess I'm wondering what's happening with us." Her gaze slid from his, almost shyly. "Ry...this is not the norm for me."

"Can you believe it's not the norm for me, either?"

Her gaze returned to his face, and she searched his eyes. After a moment she said softly, "Yes, I think I can."

He bent forward and pressed a tender kiss to her lips. Dena almost burst into tears from the emotion she sensed from him and what she herself felt during that kiss. Then Ry raised his head and looked into her eyes. "You think about it some more. I'll be sleeping in the loft tonight. The decision to join me or not is yours." He squeezed her hands, then let go of them.

She watched him walk out of the office with her heart in her throat. Placing her hand over the spot, she could feel its beat on her palm. Ry was the most special man she'd ever known. He wanted her in the most elemental way possible, had to have sensed her enormous response to his kisses, and yet he would not even attempt to pressure her into anything. He'd left it in her hands. It was her decision to make.

Another decision, she thought with a heavy sigh. She almost wished he *had* pressured her. If she hadn't been so lily-livered and worried about Nettie being in the house, they would be making love right this minute, somewhere in this office.

She paced the carpet. If she didn't go to the loft tonight, would Ry simply wash his hands of her? No, she thought, he wouldn't do that, but he would be disappointed.

Well, she was disappointed too, and unfulfilled, aching to be in his arms, longing to feel his lips on hers again. Wishing she hadn't stopped him. Overheated and with screamingly raw nerves. If she went to bed would she sleep?

What had happened here tonight was not going to vanish from her system. No, she would *not* sleep if she went to bed now.

She was not even going to try. The only man she'd ever wanted with such overwhelming desire was waiting in the barn's loft for her.

There wasn't a reason in the world to disappoint either of them.

# Ten

Dena hastened to the bathroom to refresh herself. Her hands were a bit unsteady and her heart was pounding. Going out to the loft was a bold step, quite possibly the boldest thing she had ever done. But a force stronger than ingrained inhibitions and common sense was controlling her, and it was with an uncommon breathlessness that she brushed her teeth and combed her hair. She would have liked to put on something other than the jeans she was wearing—one of the pretty new nightgowns she had purchased today would be perfect for this rendezvous—but she couldn't cross the compound in night-clothes. What was happening between her and Ry felt very private, theirs alone, and she wanted to keep it that way. If one of the men happened to wander out of the bunkhouse for a smoke or something and saw her, she didn't want him putting two and two together. He might anyway—after all, why on earth would she be heading for the barn after dark—but his curiosity would most definitely be piqued if she was wearing a seductive nightgown and robe.

She ignored lipstick, but she did lightly touch cologne to

her wrists, the base of her throat and behind her ears. In front of the mirror, she took in a long breath and looked into her own eyes. Was she really going to do this? Go out to the barn and up the ladder to the loft to meet a man for the express purpose of making love?

The answer was in her eyes. Ry wasn't just any man, and she had lived a lonely, celibate life long enough. Far too long, in fact. Maybe she had found love, maybe she hadn't. She knew her own feelings—part of the time, at least—and suspected they were genuine, but she could only guess at Ry's. And love, the kind that lasted through thick and thin, was a two-way street. It was possible he wanted her only for tonight, or maybe he anticipated an affair all during her stay in Wyoming.

But it was also possible that his expectations went deeper than a temporary relationship. And neither of them knew just how long she would be in Wyoming. He was risking his heart, just as she was.

That thought bolstered her courage, and she switched off the bathroom light and tiptoed down the hall, through the kitchen and out the back door. The crisp night air assailed her senses. She shivered slightly as she hadn't put on a jacket. She didn't run or jog, but she walked fast from the house to the barn, scanning the compound as she went to see if anyone else was out and about. She saw no one and felt relief.

Entering the barn she spotted the dim bulb burning near the loft ladder. It was a clear indication of Ry's hope that she would come, and all the excitement she had felt in his arms in the office returned to steal her breath and quicken her pulse.

"I'm over here," a deep voice said.

Dena nearly jumped out of her skin. Ry wasn't in the loft, he was in one of the dark shadows of the barn. Why? "You...you startled me," she said, her eyes darting here and there in an attempt to locate him.

Ry stepped into the faint light of the single bulb. "Sorry. That wasn't my intention." He paused then added quietly, "I wasn't sure you'd come."

She felt strangely guilty, as though she'd just been caught

with her hand in the cookie jar, and embarrassed. She'd thought he would be in bed in the loft, and now realized that an image of herself undressing in the dark had been lurking in the back of her mind. Certainly she hadn't visualized conversation before they...

She flushed hotly. Any romantic notions she'd concocted about this tryst had vanished. It hurt to think that Ry could be considering her as an easy conquest, and had absolutely no romantic feelings for her.

On the other hand, if he thought of her that way, why was he waiting for her down here instead of in the loft? She'd had every intention of climbing into bed with him, and if all he wanted from her was sex, why wasn't he in that bed on the second floor, naked and impatiently awaiting her arrival?

Confusion set in. This was so out of character for her. She knew she would not be here at all if she didn't feel something warm and alive for this man, but she could only speculate about his feelings for her. She viewed her marriage with Tommy as an abysmal failure. Maybe she hadn't become involved with a man after that because she didn't want another such downfall, or because she didn't trust her judgment of the opposite sex. How had Ry slipped through her guard? Why, even while grieving over her father, regretting the past and worrying herself sick about the future, had she permitted Ry to infiltrate her wall of self-protection?

All that flashed through her mind so fast, only a few seconds had passed since he'd said, "I wasn't sure you'd come."

"I...I came to tell you I wasn't...coming," she said, feeling a little queasy in the stomach. "I mean, I didn't want you waiting and wondering." Her voice trailed off.

Ry narrowed his eyes on her. The minute he'd walked out of the house he'd had second thoughts about this tryst. That was the reason he was on the first floor of the barn instead of up that ladder. His suggestion she come to the loft had been crude and inappropriate. Dena was a decent, moral woman and deserved respect from men, not coarse innuendo or indecent proposals. He'd intended apologizing and telling her that if she showed up. He'd even considered telling her that she was special in his eyes, the first woman he'd felt anything for since his divorce.

Now he wasn't sure of what to say. She'd come out here to tell him she wasn't coming? No, he couldn't quite believe that. She'd come to finish what they had started in the office, and he'd destroyed her mood by appearing at the foot of the loft ladder instead of being where she'd expected him to be. She had lied to recover her pride, or some damned thing, and he knew now that he had made a mistake that just might not be correctable.

He took a step toward her. "I'd like us to talk awhile."

"Uh, about what?" She was so unsure of herself right now she couldn't even speak clearly.

Ry took a moment to formulate his answer. The last thing he wanted was to scare her off, and he was afraid that blurting out how he felt about her without preamble might do just that. "Nothing earthshaking," he said with a hint of a grin that he hoped would erase that look of dismay from her face. He wanted to show her that he was at ease with the situation and so should she be. "Just a little give and take. I say something and you say something. I think you know what I mean."

Talking. Yes, maybe they should talk. Dena's mind was still going in circles, but she could see the wisdom of getting to know each other better than they did. If their relationship was going anywhere, that is. Was that what he was thinking? Hoping for? She took a nervous breath, afraid to count on that conclusion. But what a lovely thought it was. He was treating her with respect. He did not look at her as a one-night stand.

Her lips tipped at the corners in a small, tenuous smile. "Do you want this conversation to be held here?"

Ry's grin broadened. "It's not the best place for a heart-to-heart, is it? We could take a ride, if you'd like."

A vehicle starting and leaving the compound at this time of night would alert everyone on the place. "There's still the loft," she said. She wasn't sure of the topics they would be discussing, but two people could talk all night in the loft, should they choose, without anyone being the wiser.

After his brazen invitation to make love in the loft, her

suggesting they do their talking there surprised Ry. But where else could they go? Apparently she didn't want to take a ride, probably because of the way sound carried at night. Someone would be bound to hear the engine noise and ask questions. The house was out because of Nettie, so if they wished to stay indoors, it was the barn or one of the other outbuildings.

"The loft is fine with me," he said, and gestured toward the ladder. "You first."

He'd thought climbing up behind her would prevent a fall, should she slip in the dark, but she went up that ladder more nimbly than he did. "You've probably gone up and down this ladder a lot," he commented as she took the final step.

"More times than I could count." Dena stood by until Ry was next to her. There was one wall dividing the huge old loft. It hadn't been used for hay storage for many years, but it still retained the musty odor. It was darker than the first floor, but Dena knew exactly where the door to the smaller room was, and she walked unerringly toward it.

"Careful," Ry warned. He didn't want her stumbling over something.

"I know this place like my own hand," she replied.

"I'm sure you do, but there's an awful lot of old equipment and junk up here now."

"There always was," Dena said rather wryly. "And I'm sure it's worse now. The whole ranch, including the house, needs a good going-over. I'll bet we could haul a dozen truckloads of junk to the dump."

They had come to the door. Ry reached around her to find the knob. "Just say the word and I'll put the men to work on that job," he said, and pushed the door open.

The yard lights filtered through the years-old grime of the two windows on this end of the loft. Dena blinked to adjust her eyesight. Other than the small area where a bed had been set up, the entire room was crammed with boxes and pieces of furniture.

"What a godawful mess," she said disgustedly. "Is there even one thing in the entire loft that's worth keeping?"

"Not many. I've itched to clean it out since the day I started working here. But—'' He stopped, not wanting to say anything derogatory about Dena's father.

"But Dad never let you," Dena finished for him. Her gaze went to the bed. "You set the bed up. Was it already here?"

"In bits and pieces. Needed some repairs, but I took care of those and bought some new sheets and blankets." He paused, then added, "I like to be alone sometimes."

"And this is where you come." She smiled. "Not in winter, though, I'd bet."

He smiled too. "No, not during freezing weather. But it's great on summer nights."

"Like tonight."

All this time they had been standing just inside the room, only inches apart. Ry had been inhaling her cologne and was so aware of her nearness, he was beginning to feel choked. Coming up here to do their talking had not been the wisest move. They were so alone, and it was so quiet he could almost hear her heart beating. Without question he could hear his own. What had he wanted to talk to her about, anyway? He couldn't seem to put it all together now with his mind so full of her and that delectable perfume she was wearing.

Dena was realizing there was nowhere to sit. Other than the bed, of course. There were probably some old chairs in the heaps of junk crowding the room, but anyone digging them out would get dirty, and besides, if there were chairs they'd undoubtedly be broken and unusable.

"Well," she said, turning to look at Ry. Even in the dim light she could see the way he was looking at her, and her heart leapt into her throat. Statue still, they stood there with locked gazes until the very air around them reeked of sexual tension.

Then, suddenly, they were in each other's arms. "Dena," Ry whispered hoarsely before pressing his lips to hers. It was a hard, passionate kiss, a hungry kiss, and it was as though no time at all had elapsed from their kisses in the office until this moment. All the thoughts and ideas they had each debated in their own minds downstairs were gone, replaced with pure sensation. With desire, and overwhelming need of each other.

In all of Dena's adult life she had not felt as she did now, and her hands roamed and groped as wildly as Ry's. One gasping kiss blended into another and another. She unbuttoned his shirt and heard his groan when her hands explored his bare chest. He removed her blouse and buried his face into the cleavage of her breasts. Her legs got weak and she clung to him for support.

"You smell so good," he whispered raggedly. "Like wildflowers on a sunny day." He picked her up and carried her to the bed.

She went willingly, so thrilled and excited she thought she might burst. The flames in her body were hotter than any she'd ever experienced, way beyond anything she'd thought possible. A euphoric sense of utter freedom overrode her every worry, care and problem. Tomorrow was soon enough to return to the real world; tonight was hers.

"Ah," she said on a seductive sigh as Ry lowered her to the bed.

He sat next to her, put one hand on the pillow beside her head and leaned over her to look into her eyes. She looked back without shyness or modesty.

"You're very beautiful," he said in a low, husky voice.

This time she didn't disagree, maybe because she felt beautiful. And womanly, very, very womanly. There were so many degrees to femininity and masculinity, and she wasn't always aware of her femaleness. Right now she felt more feminine than at any time of her life, and Ry seemed to be the epitome of strong, handsome and desirable maleness.

"You're quite beautiful yourself," she said, garnering a smile from Ry.

Then his smile slowly slipped away as he took his hand from the pillow and began touching her, running his fingers down her arm and back up to her shoulder. He dipped his head to kiss her, and said just before their lips met, "I never thought there was anything missing in my life until I met you."

His kiss prevented a reply from her, but with closed eyes and extreme pleasure mounting in her body, she thought that was probably the nicest thing a man had ever said to her. It warmed her soul and heightened her feelings for him. If she hadn't been falling in love with him before this, she was certainly doing so now. Her arms rose to encircle his neck, and she kissed him back with all of the passion and love she was feeling.

He pleased her further by not hurrying their lovemaking. His caresses were tender and slowly paced, and he seemed as enchanted with the curve of her throat as he was with her breasts. He stopped kissing her mouth to kiss her tummy, then gently removed her bra. She pushed his shirt from his shoulders, and he shook himself free of it.

It was like a lovely dance. Between kisses that were alternately fiery and tender, they shed the rest of their clothing with no awkwardness whatsoever. At some point Ry got them under the covers. *Oh, my love,* she thought dreamily, snuggling into his arms.

They held each other like that for several wonderful minutes, but the sensation of bare skin against bare skin, of intertwined arms and legs, and the wonder of being in bed together refueled their desire. Once again kisses were necessary to life itself, and now they explored each other's body without the barrier of clothing.

"Oh, Ry," Dena whispered, and again, "Oh!" when his hand slid between her legs. She tensed.

Ry spoke softly into her ear. "The first time a man and woman are together is all guesswork. You have to tell me if I do something you don't like."

She swallowed. It was just that no one had touched her in that especially private place since her marriage, and though she'd thought herself prepared for anything with Ry tonight, her natural instinct had been to recoil at that particular intimacy.

"I will," she whispered, and to show him she was ready for this, she relaxed her thighs and let them fall open. When he kissed her again, she held nothing in reserve, not even a tiny part of herself just in case this never went beyond tonight.

It was a hell of a risk for a woman like her. She knew it,

too, giving everything to a man who'd sworn off marriage for good. She'd taken almost the same vow, but hers had been tempered with *I will only marry again if I meet the perfect man*.

Well, no one was perfect, but Ry Hardin was darned close. She was already feeling emotionally committed to him, and if he didn't reciprocate, she could be in for some big-time heartache.

But what else was new? Wasn't she so used to heartache she wouldn't know how to behave if it should suddenly disappear?

In the next heartbeat she wasn't thinking about anything. Ry's fingers were lifting her to a whole new plane of pleasure. Her body moved in rhythmic response while heat radiated throughout her system. Her breath came in short gasps and the blood raced through her veins.

But the pressure was mounting, she was on the brink and she didn't want it to happen like this. "Wait," she said breathlessly, taking his hand in hers to still its movement. "I...I want...I'd rather..." It wasn't easy to say, and she couldn't quite find the right words.

She didn't have to. Ry understood. When he'd pulled back the blankets he had slipped a small foil packet under his pillow. Now he retrieved it, tore it open and put on the condom. He hated those things but knew they were necessary and never failed to use them. His one exception had been during the first months of his short-lived marriage because he'd hoped so much for a child. But things had started going downhill, and he'd learned that Kate had been using her own brand of birth control all the while. And not only with him.

He shook those old memories from his head. They didn't hurt anymore, but this was not the time to be thinking of the past. Dena was not Kate. Dena was like no woman he'd ever known. A shocking truth came in a blinding flash: *I'm in love with her!*

He didn't tell her because it was something he needed to think about. Not now. Later, when he was alone and could think straight. But his heart was beating faster, there was a roaring in his head because of it, and he wanted her even more than he had because of it.

Moving on top of her, he supported most of his weight on his elbows and probed the depths of her eyes, looking for answers to questions that had suddenly become crucial. *Why are you doing this? Do you love me too?*

Unaware of the profundity of his thoughts, Dena wrapped her legs around his hips and drew his head down to kiss his incredible mouth. "Do it," she whispered against his lips. "I need you. Oh, I need you so much." The need was a living thing within her, a yearning so commanding and powerful that it made her a totally different woman than she'd ever been. She writhed under him until his manhood was within the vee of her thighs, exactly where she wanted it. Then, wantonly, she moved so that there was a delicious friction between them.

Ry's blood pressure shot through the roof. He forgot about keeping his weight off her and burrowed his hands under her hips to lift her into the perfect position for entry. She arched and gasped as he slid into her. The heat of his tumescence seared her, its size stretched and filled her, and the yearning within her became a wild and untamed thing.

"Ry," she cried, digging her fingertips into his back.

Alarmed, he stopped moving. She was small and he was so big. "Am I hurting you?"

"No, oh, no," she moaned. "It's good, so good."

He sucked in a ragged breath of relief. If she had asked him to stop, he would have and then endured the painful aftermath without resentment. She eased his concern further by whispering, "Nothing's ever been so good."

He took her face in his hands and searched her eyes. Was she actually telling him that her pleasure with him surpassed her experiences with any other man? "Nothing?" he asked, his voice husky and emotional.

"Nothing," she said so softly he could barely hear her.

Passion and pride rose within him, constricting his chest, clogging his throat. Placing his forearms on the pillow on each side of her head, he began moving again, this time watching her face with all of the intensity of his feelings. When her lids drooped, he whispered gutturally, "Open your eyes. Let me see what you're feeling."

She complied, and realized after a minute why he had made that request. Looking into the eyes of a lover was not only emotionally bonding, it raised her sense of intimacy to a level she hadn't known existed. Breathing hard, she dampened her lips with the tip of her tongue. She felt sweaty and overheated, and Ry's eyes were so dark and hot looking, she knew he felt the same.

His thrusts began to go deeper. She emitted a low groan with each one, and moved her hips to rise and fall with his.

"Dena," he whispered. "If you only knew..."

She couldn't even ask what he meant. In fact, his words fell on deaf ears. She was so lost in sensation, so deeply immersed in pleasure, that the walls might have caved in and she wouldn't have known it. Or cared.

Her hands caressed the contours of his damp back, then his buttocks. She marveled at the rippling under his skin that occurred each time he plunged into her, the tightening and relaxing of muscle and sinew.

Then, like a wave appearing on the sea and coming closer, she felt the beginning of the end. She clutched Ry more tightly and said his name again and again. Her head moved back and forth on the pillow, and tears gathered in her eyes.

Recognizing the signs, Ry let himself go. Everything went a little crazy for a few minutes. The bed rocked noisily with their frenetic movements. Thoughts were nonexistent. Words were whispered that neither used in everyday circumstances.

"Yes...oh, yes," Dena cried out as the spasms of release began and grew stronger in the pit of her stomach. She clawed at his back and sought his mouth with hers.

There was one brief but frantic kiss before the final explosion. "Dena!" Ry shouted.

She clung to him until her body was weak and trembling. Tears ran down her temples to the pillow, and one sob rose in her throat and broke the ensuing silence.

Ry was limp as a dishrag, but that sob worried him. He

lifted his head to see her. "Is anything wrong? Are you all right?"

She smiled through her tears and lovingly touched his face. "I have never been better in my life."

The tension created by that sob relaxed from his face. "Dena, if that's really the truth..." He realized that he was again on the verge of telling her he was in love with her and had to clamp his lips shut to keep from doing so. There was no reason to rush that part of their relationship. She was still grieving her father's death. She had Simon's estate and its tax ramifications to deal with. She'd given him tonight; he shouldn't ask for more. Far better that he let nature take its course, probably for him as well as for her. After all, he'd never expected to fall in love again, had never even *hoped* it would happen. And though there were a lot of indications that she was falling in love with him, too, he thought it best they move along slowly in that direction.

He gently brushed a tendril of hair from her forehead. "If I take a little walk, will you wait here for me? We never did have that talk."

Smiling, she nodded. "I'll be here."

He kissed her sensually swollen lips, then scooted from the bed. Yanking on only his jeans, he strode from the room.

Dena stretched as lazily as a cat, then pulled the sheet and blankets over her. For a while she smiled into the gloom of the room, totally contented.

But then, out of the blue, she thought of her father, and how strongly he would have disapproved of her behavior tonight. Her smile faded and her stomach began churning.

She couldn't bear lying there and thinking about it. Jumping out of bed, she hurriedly pulled on her clothes and raced from the room to the ladder. Ry was just starting up it and couldn't believe his eyes.

"Are you leaving?" he asked incredulously.

"I...yes." Turning, she started down the ladder. Ry backed down the few rungs he'd taken to wait at the foot for her. Mass confusion reigned in his mind. What had happened in the space of five minutes to cause this?

She took the last step and stood on ground level. "Dena, what's wrong?" Ry asked. He laid his hands on her shoulders and peered into her face. "Tell me, please."

"I...can't." She didn't want him to know what she'd done to her father. "Ry, it has nothing to do with you, but I...I really can't stay any longer."

"Nor can you talk about it," he said in a truly saddened voice.

Dena's heart nearly broke. Hurting Ry was the last thing she wanted to do, but there was so much he didn't know, and she couldn't tell him about it, and she had so much to deal with that didn't concern him, and she couldn't talk about that, either.

"I'm sorry," she said with tears in her eyes. Slipping from his grasp, she backed away. "Good night."

Nearly weeping himself, Ry watched her go. Then he took a breath and called, "This isn't over, Dena. Don't think it is."

She left the barn with her head down. He was right. She'd fallen in love with him and it would never be over.

# Eleven

Dena awoke the next morning groggy and tired. Her mind had been active all during the night, disrupting her sleep again and again. There were bitter undertones to her mood; she couldn't even fall in love with a wonderful man without worrying about how her father might have perceived her conduct. Was this to be the norm for the rest of her life? If so, she was going to grow old alone and very lonely.

And what if Ry should become irritated over her erratic behavior with him and leave the ranch? What would she do without him? She would wither away to nothing if he wasn't around. Somehow she would manage the ranch's operation, or make that decision to sell out. But the ranch's care was no longer her uppermost concern. It was how she felt about Ry, and how he felt about her. It was their incredible lovemaking, his touch on her body, his kisses, his tenderness and passion.

A question struck her in the shower: Would things fall into place with Ry if she got the uncertainties of the other portions of her life straightened out? It was something she had to do, anyway, and maybe if she forced herself to buckle down and make the decisions that had to be made, she would be able to stop regretting and lamenting the past and look to the future with some modicum of anticipation.

Tears suddenly stung her eyes. If only she could forget what she'd done to her father. If only she could forget what *he* had done to her. It wasn't impossible to summon an image of her and Ry as man and wife, happy and running the ranch together, maybe putting in that irrigation system he believed to be important. It was just so unlikely with irreparable heartache constantly eating at her.

She had to at least *try* to make things right. She would begin today, she decided with a sigh and a silent prayer for wisdom and strength.

She put on one of her new outfits instead of her usual jeans, a pretty but casual blue and white dress and white sandals. With her hair arranged and makeup on her face, she went to the kitchen.

Nettie's eyes lit up. "Well, don't you look nice! My, that dress is becoming. I just love those long, flowing skirts."

"Thank you, Nettie. I'm going to eat a bite, make some phone calls and then drive to Winston. Would you like to come along?"

"Oh, honey, I'd love to go, but I've got bread dough rising and apples all peeled and sliced for pies. Some other day, okay?"

Dena poured herself a glass of orange juice and dropped a slice of bread into the toaster. "I would have given you some warning, but my plans only gelled this morning."

"Don't you worry about it one iota. We'll do it another time." Nettie placed her hands on her hips. "Dena, is that all you're having for breakfast?"

"I'm not hungry, Nettie. Toast and juice are all I want." There were many things on her mind; food was not one of them. Her shower had revitalized her energy, but it was the decision she'd made to dive headfirst into her problems that really had her system percolating. She was anxious to get started.

Nettie clucked disapprovingly. She had always thought

breakfast to be the most important meal of the day, which she'd told Dena many times during her teen years when Dena had been rushing around getting ready for school and grabbing an orange or a piece of toast instead of sitting at the table and eating a normal breakfast.

Dena couldn't help smiling. Nettie's steadfastness was comforting; not everything in this crazy world was topsy-turvy.

With her plate of toast and glass of orange juice, Dena went to the office and sat at the desk. After eating, she dialed Meditech in Seattle. Before anything else, she had to touch base with her employer. Gail answered, as expected, and immediately began asking questions. "When are you coming back?" "Is everything all right there?" "How've you been doing?"

Dena fielded Gail's curiosity the best she could, then changed the subject. "Is Mr. Decker in?"

"He is right now, but you're lucky you called when you did. He's been running back and forth between this place and Meditech's new office across town, so I never know when he'll be here. Hold on and I'll put you through."

Dena took a nervous breath. Larry Decker wasn't an ogre by any means, but he wasn't the easiest person to talk to, either. He was *all* business, and when he decided someone was more liability than asset to his operation, he let him or her go without a qualm. Dena didn't want that tie broken yet. If everything went to pot here, in Wyoming, she would want to return to Seattle, and she would probably also want to resume her duties with Meditech. More than likely she would end up with some money from the estate, but she had no idea what the ranch was worth, and she'd been warned about the high percentage of federal taxes that could be due on it. She certainly wasn't counting on great wealth, whether she kept the ranch or sold out, and burning her bridges with Meditech seemed foolhardy to her.

A male voice came on the line. "Dena?"

"Hello, Mr. Decker. The reason I called..."

"You're not still in Wyoming, are you?" He sounded disgruntled.

"I—I'm afraid I'm going to have to stay here for a while longer."

"How much longer?"

"I'm not sure. Is that a problem?"

"Damned right it's a problem. We've been running short-handed without you, and with the second office opening in two weeks, things aren't exactly calm around here. You're going to have to give me some idea of when you'll be back."

It wasn't an unfair request; an employer had the right to expect his employees to be on the job. But Dena was in no mood to be pinned down like this.

"My situation is far from ordinary, Mr. Decker," she said, speaking with more firmness than before. "I'd be only too happy to give you the precise date of my return, if there was one. There's not. I won't bore you with the details of all the loose ends with my father's estate, and I apologize for my extended absence, but I simply can't pull a date out of the air. I hope you understand."

"I hope *you* understand my position, Dena. I'm going to have to replace you. You know how busy this office is and how tight our schedules are. Let's agree to do this. When you're ready to come back to Seattle, give me a call. If nothing else, you can work relief until a full-time opening comes up."

Dena slumped back in the chair. "You're letting me go, then," she said dully.

"I have no choice, Dena. I'm sorry because you've been with us for a long time and you're an exceptionally good nurse. I sympathize with your situation, but I cannot permit employees' personal problems to interfere with the operation of this company. Dena, I have another call. Contact me when you return to Seattle. Goodbye." He hung up.

After putting down the phone, Dena rubbed her temples. Tension and disappointment were giving her a headache. "Damn," she whispered. Now she was out of a job. It was not the result she had hoped for from that call.

Hurt and angry in spite of knowing that Decker was only doing his job, she grabbed the phone again and placed another long distance call to Seattle. The manager of her apartment complex answered. "Mrs. Potter, this is Dena Colby."

"Yes, Dena, how are you?"

"I'm fine, Mrs. Potter. Listen, I know my mail must be piling up. Could I impose on you to box it up and send it to me? I'll reimburse you for the cost, of course."

"I'll take care of it today."

"Sort through it, if you would, and send only what looks important."

"Are you keeping the apartment, Dena?"

"Yes, I am. You'll receive a check for the rent on the first of the month, as usual. Here's my mailing address, Mrs. Potter." Dena recited the ranch's address. "I'm going to the post office today to have my mail forwarded, so if anything arrives in the interim, just write that address on the envelope with a 'Please Forward' notice. Also, let me know the cost of mailing my things and I'll get a check out to you immediately."

"Very well."

"I can't thank you enough, Mrs. Potter. I know I must have some bills in my mail that need payment."

"You're welcome, Dena. I hope things are going well for you."

Dena sighed silently. "Everything's fine, Mrs. Potter. I just have to be here much longer than I'd initially thought. Goodbye."

Dena's next call was another disappointment: Terry Endicott was out for the day. His receptionist said cheerfully, "Mr. Endicott accommodates several clients by going to their place of business on a regular basis. Shall I have him call you tomorrow?"

"I'll call him. Thank you." Dena hung up.

Sitting back, Dena drummed her fingertips on the top of the desk. Maybe John Chandler had the results of Ellen's appraisal, which was what she had wanted to ask Terry Endicott, and since she was already going to Winston to make that change of address, she might as well drop in on Mr. Chandler and find out what he knew. It was time they met, anyway.

He could be out, too, she thought wryly while getting to

her feet. But she wasn't going to call for an appointment. If he wasn't in, she would see him another day.

She brought her plate and glass to the kitchen and put them in the dishwasher. "I'm leaving now, Nettie."

"Have a nice day, honey."

Dena went to her bedroom for her purse, then left the house through the front door. She was heading for the car she intended taking to Winston when she heard a vehicle approaching the ranch via the long driveway. She stood and watched it drive in. It was a low-slung, bright red sports car, a beautiful automobile, and it screeched to a halt right next to her.

Her jaw dropped when she saw the driver: Tommy!

He got out with a lazy grin and patted the hood of the car. "Hi, Dena. What d'ya think of this baby?"

"Hello, Tommy. It's gorgeous. Whose is it?"

"It's mine." There was pride all over Tommy's handsome face.

"Yours!"

"Yup, all mine. How about taking a ride? This baby really moves."

Dena was dying to know how he could afford a "baby" like this, but she wasn't going to take a ride with Tommy to find out.

"Sorry," she said, "but I have things to do. I was getting ready to leave when you drove in."

Ry had just happened to walk out of the barn at the same time Dena went to her car. He'd stopped to admire her in that dress and was all set to jog over and tell her how beautiful she looked, when the sports car arrived. A tall, young man got out of it, and Ry could tell that Dena knew him. Frowning, he leaned against the corral fence to watch. While Dena and the stranger talked, Ry's stomach churned uneasily. Who was that guy? An old friend? A new friend? Damn!

"Aw, come on, Dena," Tommy pleaded. "It ain't every day that a man gets a car like this. Take a ride with me." His tone of voice changed. "You always were the prettiest girl in the county, and you still are. You couldn't have forgotten how it was with us."

"You're right," she said with a raised eyebrow. "I haven't forgotten a thing."

Tommy had the grace to flush, but he recovered quickly. "I'm talking about how it was at first. I know things went wrong, but hell, honey, we were just a couple of kids. We're not kids anymore, and I know now how a woman likes to be treated."

"Do you really?" Dena drawled.

Tommy grinned. "Give me the chance and I'll prove it."

Gritting his teeth, Ry wondered just how long that conversation was going to go on. There was some distance between him and Dena, but she didn't look at all unhappy to him.

"Tommy, you'll never change," Dena said with a laugh she couldn't prevent. She didn't hate her ex-husband, although all of that charm he was throwing around was wasted on her. Next to Ry, Tommy was a boy, and he would rely on his looks to get what he wanted for as long as they lasted.

"I'll never change about some things. One of those things is that I never stopped missing you," Tommy said with an exaggerated expression of a lost and lonely man.

Dena laughed again. "Which was the reason you remarried, right?"

"No, but it was why the marriage didn't last. I tried to forget you, but she knew, Dena, she knew you were always on my mind."

"Tommy, you're so full of bull it's a wonder it's not coming out of your ears. Look, I really do have to go." Dena reached for door handle of her car.

"Where're you going? Let me drive you there, wherever it is. We can talk and get to know each other again. Honey, give me another chance. I still love you. I always will. We never should have gotten divorced."

She stared at him in amazement. "You can't be serious."

Tommy moved closer and tried to take her hand. "I've never been more serious about anything."

Dena avoided the hand holding by taking a backward step. What game was he playing? Dare she believe him? It wasn't that she cared one way or the other, as her teenage infatuation with Tommy Hogan had vanished long ago. But she had no desire to hurt him, and if he really was still in love with her, she wanted to let him down easy.

Opening the door of her car, she tossed her purse on the front seat, then turned to face Tommy again. "What do you want from me, Tommy?"

His boyish grin flashed. "For now, a ride in my new car."

Dena folded her arms across her chest and leaned against the front fender of her own car. "And then what?"

He laughed, took the few steps between them and flirtatiously chucked her under the chin. "What do you think?"

Dena unfolded her arms and slapped his hand away. It was astounding that he thought they could reassemble the shambles of their marriage. He never would grow up, would he? Waltzing in here with his new car to impress her, then hoping to impress her further by telling her he loved her.

Dena eyed the gleaming sports car. "How did you afford to buy a car like this?" she asked. Maybe he had a good job now, but if so it had happened awfully fast, and much too recently to have built credit or saved wages for this kind of purchase.

He slid his hands into his pants pockets and looked as proud as a peacock. "My family bought it for me."

Dena's gaze jerked from the car to him, incredulity and doubt on every feature of her face. "You mean they pooled their resources to buy you an expensive car?" In her memory the Hogans had not been generous people. True, they hadn't had much with which to *be* generous back then, but try as she might, she could not visualize the family getting together, deciding that Tommy just had to have a sports car, then digging into meager savings accounts and throwing the money into a pot.

But maybe things had changed for the Hogans, and their savings were no longer meager. Ellen had a good job; maybe some of the others did, as well.

Regardless of improved financial worth, if that was the case, Dena still couldn't picture the Hogan family single-minded on any subject, particularly one that hit them in their pocketbooks.

"They sure did," Tommy said, still beaming with pride.

There was another witness to this little tableau besides Ry. Nettie, too, had heard the car arriving, and had gone to a front window of the house to see who had come along. She'd watched Tommy and Dena with pursed lips for a while, then returned to her work in the kitchen, shaking her head over the infamous Hogan gall. That was when she noticed Ry standing at the corral, also watching Tommy and Dena.

"Well, well," she murmured. "So that's the lay of the land these days."

Ry didn't see Nettie at the kitchen window looking at him as his eyes and mind were focused on Dena and the guy with the sports car. Ry's stomach got tighter with each passing minute, and every time that jerk tried to touch Dena, he wanted to go over there and bust him one in the chops.

But he didn't own Dena Colby, and hadn't he learned years ago that love was no more than a kick in the pants? Hadn't he sworn off commitment after his divorce? How had he let Dena get so close that he'd forgotten everything he'd vowed and fallen in love again? Curses ran through his mind, directed at his own foolish thoughts and behavior. Thank God he hadn't blurted out his feelings last night.

Dena couldn't keep her curiosity bottled up another second. "Why?" she asked Tommy. "Why would your family pool their money and buy you a car, especially a car like this?"

"'Cause they love me," Tommy quipped. "Why else?"

Yes, indeed, why else? thought Dena. The conjecture made her feel uneasy, as though she was part of some nefarious scheme of the Hogans. Shaking off the discomfiting thought, she moved to the door of her car and opened it again.

"I have to go," she said, and slid behind the wheel.

Tommy held the door open and leaned into the car. "So you're not going to take that ride with me?"

"Definitely not. Please don't ask again."

"Will you go out with me tonight?"

Her eyes widened. "Of course I won't go out with you! Why would you even think such a thing?"

"I told you why, sweetheart. I still love you. Doesn't that

mean anything to you? Don't my feelings count at all?'' He looked so sad and disheartened that Dena felt sorry for him.

She spoke more gently. ''Tommy, you said it yourself. We were kids during our marriage. We weren't in love, we were infatuated.'' *I grew up, you didn't.* ''Tommy, there's no chance of a reconciliation, not in a romantic way. You have to accept that.''

He looked on the verge of tears. ''No, Dena, I don't, and I won't. It all came rushing back when I saw you at the funeral. I'll never give up on us, honey, never. We belong together, we always have, and someday you'll know it, too.''

She was suddenly nervous—maybe she'd seen too many movies about stalkers and obsessive lovers—and gave a little laugh to cover it. ''I have to be going, Tommy. Please let go of the door.''

He looked at her for a long moment then nodded. ''I'll be back,'' he said, and closed her door. Then he smiled, and Dena was struck again by how handsome he was.

But good looks weren't enough. She would never go out with Tommy, or give him one single reason to hope for a reconciliation.

She started the engine, and he stepped back from her car. As she drove away she saw him jump into the sports car. He was right behind her as she traversed the driveway to the highway.

Ry caught himself chewing on his bottom lip. Every muscle in his body was taut with tension. They'd left in different vehicles, but he would bet anything a rendezvous was in the making.

That idea hurt so much he turned around and punched a post in the corral fence. After that he walked away with an aching fist and an even more painful ache in his chest.

So much for love, he thought bitterly. So damned much.

The sports car stayed on Dena's tail all the way to Winston. Every time she looked into the rearview mirror and saw it, she grew tenser. By the time she pulled into a parking space in

front of the post office, she was ready to give Tommy a piece
of her mind.

He didn't give her the chance. Tooting his horn, waving
and grinning, he drove on by. She watched with a scathing,
angry expression as the sleek, cherry red car disappeared down
the street. Tommy was *not* going to follow and haunt her,
dammit, even if it meant obtaining a restraining order against
him. The Hogans would hate her more than they already did,
but so be it.

She marched into the post office, took care of the change
of address notice, then marched back out to her car. She was
about to get in when she heard her name being called. Turning,
she suddenly felt as wilted as last week's lettuce. Coming toward her with a huge smile on her face was Tommy's mother.

"Dena, honey, how are you?" Karen Hogan trilled. "My,
you look just beautiful in that dress. You didn't buy it in
Winston, did you? Looks expensive, and much too stylish for
any of our little shops."

Tommy's facial features resembled his mother's. Although
Karen was overweight, she was a pretty woman. Actually,
Dena had always thought all the Hogans to be physically attractive people. It was their belief that the world owed them
a living and their constant attempts to get something for nothing that had driven Dena up the wall.

"I'm fine," Dena answered slowly, ignoring the comments
on her looks and dress. Karen hadn't been this friendly when
Dena had been her daughter-in-law. What was going on?
"How are you?" The question was an automatic response.
She really did not want to hear the state of Karen's health or
financial situation, either of which Dena knew Karen was perfectly capable of discoursing upon for hours on end.

Karen sighed. "Not very well, I'm afraid. I have a bad
heart, honey. Dr. Worth said I have to take it real easy."

"I'm sorry to hear that," Dena murmured. Her sympathy
on that score was genuine. Even though resenting the Hogan
family, she didn't wish any of them ill health. To her surprise
Karen got tears in her eyes, and was looking at Dena as though
she were a long-lost daughter.

"I can't tell you how much the family has missed you, Dena," the older woman said sadly. "We were all so sorry to hear about your father's death. We talked and talked about whether we should attend his funeral, and then Tommy volunteered to go and represent the Hogans. He's so thoughtful that way." Karen's teary smile conveyed pride in her son's thoughtfulness. "Always thinking of everyone but himself."

Dena nearly swallowed her teeth. If Tommy put *anyone* ahead of himself these days, he'd certainly done a lot of changing, which she doubted with every fiber of her being. This conversation was a farce, and she couldn't stand there and be a part of it any longer.

"I really have to get going, Karen." Dena began backing away.

Karen looked disappointed. "I do hope we run into each other again."

Smiling weakly, Dena opened the door of her car. "I'm sure it's inevitable."

"Let's *make* it inevitable," Karen said with sudden good cheer. "Come to the house on Saturday for dinner. I'll get the family together, and we'll have a barbecue. Everyone will be so thrilled to see you."

Dena's heart sank. If she weaseled out of Saturday by citing other plans, Karen would suggest another day. There was no way to elude the invitation other than a flat-out refusal.

She took a breath. "Karen, I really don't think that's a good idea." A flash of inspiration struck her. "I'm very involved with someone, and he takes up all my free time."

Karen's face fell. "Who's the lucky man?" she asked with a sneer.

Dena blinked. Now she was seeing the Karen she remembered, and the woman's quick change of attitude threw Dena for a moment. Something *was* going on. Tommy showing up at the ranch with that fancy car and Karen fawning all over her until she mentioned another man definitely indicated a scheme of some sort to Dena. A scheme aimed at her. Good heavens, why?

"You don't know him," Dena said quietly. "Goodbye,

Karen.'' She slid behind the wheel, pulled the door shut and started the engine. She drove away from the post office without looking back. Her heart was thudding with dread. The Hogans were plotting something that included her, but what was it? And why would they bother? Good Lord, after the lies with which they'd blanketed the area following the divorce, how did they have the nerve to even speak to her?

John Chandler's office was only a few streets over from the post office, and it took Dena no more than five minutes to get there and park. She got out of the car and strode to the building with a heavy heart and a frown. Figuring out the Hogans was impossible, and in all honesty their attention and friendliness scared the tar out of her. They were phony, dishonest people, and there was very little she would put past them.

The legal office was on the second floor of a lovely old house. The first floor was divided into two units, one occupied by an insurance agent and the other by a real estate company. Dena climbed the carpeted stairs and found herself in a spacious, nicely decorated reception area. A woman seated at a large desk smiled at her.

"Hello," the woman said.

"Mrs. Parks?"

"Yes, and you're…?"

"Dena Colby. Is Mr. Chandler in?"

"Yes, he is, and I know he'll be pleased to see you. Just a moment." She picked up the phone and punched a number. "John, Dena Colby is here." After a second she said, "Very well."

She had no more than put down the phone when a door opened and a man came through it. He was in his middle fifties, Dena estimated, and had graying black hair and a wonderful smile. "Dena, at last we meet. I'm very glad you dropped in." He walked over to Dena and offered his hand. After their handshake, he said, "Come into my office. Would you like a cup of coffee?"

"Could I have a glass of water?" Her mouth was dry, probably a residual effect from that startling meeting with Karen Hogan.

"Indeed you may."

"I'll get it," Sheila Parks said.

"Come," John Chandler said to Dena. "Sheila will bring your water." He ushered Dena into his office and brought her to a corner arrangement of blue leather sofa and two matching chairs. There were tables and lamps, as well, a very pleasant area in what was obviously a business office as the rest of the room contained a massive oak desk and credenza, walls of law books and a computer and printer. The desktop was strewn with papers and file folders.

"Please sit down," John said to her.

They chose their places, Dena in one of the chairs, the lawyer on the sofa. He leaned back. "How are you doing?"

Dena sensed this man's kindly nature, and that she could trust him. She heaved a sigh and relaxed enough to be honest. "Not very well, I'm afraid."

"Things aren't going well at the ranch?"

"That's not it, Mr. Chandler. Dad had good men at the ranch, and they're doing their jobs. I just can't seem to get... oriented."

"Well, losing a parent is a traumatic experience, Dena."

"May I ask you something?"

"Of course."

"Did Dad ever tell you why he included me in the trust?"

The lawyer frowned. "I'm afraid I don't understand your question, Dena. Why wouldn't he include his only child?"

"Then he never explained our background?"

John took a moment to think. He shook his head. "I don't recall a conversation of that nature, no."

Dena looked down at her hands fidgeting with her purse. "He never told you that he hadn't spoken one word to me since I was eighteen years old?" The attorney's long silence was answer enough. Somehow, gossip on that subject had eluded him. She raised her eyes. "You didn't know, did you?"

"No, Dena," John said gently. "I didn't know. I'm sorry. But now I understand your question."

Sheila Parks came in with a tray containing bottled water

and two glasses. Smiling at Dena, she set the tray on the coffee table. "There you are," she murmured.

"Thank you," Dena said.

"Thanks, Sheila," John echoed. Mrs. Parks nodded and left. John filled the two glasses with cool water and handed one to Dena. While she drank, he said quietly, "All of this must be quite a shock for you."

Dena lowered her glass. "It is." She took another swallow of water and added, "I'm not sure what to do about it."

"You were hoping Simon had explained his actions to me. Dena, a man doesn't leave his property to a daughter he doesn't love. Hasn't that occurred to you?"

"Yes, but it's not logical."

"Emotions aren't always logical, Dena."

She appreciated his attempts to comfort her, but he knew no more about Simon's motivation for including her in the trust than she did. It was disappointing but, given her father's reticent nature, not surprising. She changed the subject.

"Have you heard if Ellen Clark finished her appraisal of the ranch? I called Terry Endicott this morning, but he's out for the day. I thought maybe you might have some information about it."

John shook his head. "I don't look for it for a week or so, Dena. Mrs. Clark turns in professional packages when she does an appraisal. You see, a personal inspection of the property in question is only the first step of an appraisal. There's also a title search to be done, and scouting out information on as many comparable properties recently sold or on the market as she can locate. She checks with the tax assessor's office, and...well, suffice it to say that it's quite a process."

"It appears so," Dena said slowly.

John peered at her with a curious eye. "Have you been wondering about the monetary value of what you inherited?"

"It's not that as much as wanting to get the estate settled. I have some rather crucial decisions to make, and I'd like to get that tax business out of the way as quickly as possible."

"I see. Well, I can tell you this much, even without Ellen Clark's appraisal. You're going to be hit pretty hard in the tax department. The ranch is worth at least three million dollars, and Simon had another two million in liquid assets. Plus there's a million-dollar life insurance policy, naming you as beneficiary."

Dena was so shocked she couldn't speak. Even breathing was difficult. She felt dazed, unable to think clearly. Six million dollars? John Chandler was talking about *six million dollars?*

"You had no idea?" John asked. "Terry could have told you the same thing, or you might have been able to figure it out from Simon's personal records, depending on how thorough they are. The estate taxes will eat up a lot of the cash, Dena, maybe most of it, but you're still going to be a very wealthy young woman." Seeing her white face and startled eyes, he added, "I'm sorry, Dena, I thought you knew."

"I...didn't," she said weakly. "I...didn't."

# Twelve

Dena drove slowly as she couldn't keep her mind on the road. Her tasks in town were over and she was heading home, but she would have been leaving Winston even if she'd had a list of things left to do. The shock John Chandler had delivered was still with her, making her grip the steering wheel so tightly her knuckles were white.

It was early afternoon and the sun was bright in a brilliant blue sky with a handful of puffy white clouds floating along on a high breeze, but Dena's thoughts were not on the scenery or the perfect weather. They were on money, and memories, and love, and all the complexities of her life. One question kept repeating itself: was a multimillion-dollar inheritance proof that her father *had* loved her? She liked neither the question nor the feeling it gave her: equating money with love was crass and upsetting. One forgiving word from Simon would have far outweighed any amount of money or even finding herself in possession of his beloved Wind River Ranch.

Had any other person ever gotten so heartsick over a parent's rejection? she asked herself with a sickish feeling in her stomach. Simon's censure had been extreme, but still, had *she* overreacted? There was no question that the past had ruled her life since the day she'd walked out of the house to marry Tommy. Not at first. Maybe she hadn't really believed that Simon had meant to keep his vow of silence, or maybe she'd been too wrapped up in the brand-new excitement of being a wife: she and Tommy living on their own, making love, giggling together over silly jokes, eating junk food and running here and there on whatever whim hit them, had kept them too busy to worry about her father's stern attitude.

After a few months the novelty had worn off and she'd started grasping the seriousness and responsibility of adulthood and marriage. There was rent to pay and food to buy, and a visit to Dr. Worth was a major calamity as they had no medical insurance. Tommy had changed jobs like other men changed shirts, and every time he quit another one, Dena had gotten a little more uneasy and insecure. Now she wondered if through it all she'd felt her father would be there if things got too bad. Would she have asked him for rent money, for example, if she hadn't been able to scrape together enough money to pay it some month?

It had been a terrible blow the day she had finally driven out to the ranch with reconciliation in mind and he had walked out of the house when she'd gone in. From that day forward her greatest goal had been to regain his good graces.

It hadn't happened, and now he was dead and it would *never* happen.

Still, maybe she had overreacted. Perhaps other people in her situation wrote off their recalcitrant parent and went on with their own lives. It had never occurred to her to even try to do that. Instead she had fretted and written letters and made calls to the ranch. For years. Until Ry had contacted her with the news of Simon's death.

And while Simon had been ignoring her and acting as though he had no children at all, he'd been planning to make her a wealthy woman. It made no sense to Dena, though it touched her so deeply she had to keep wiping away tears.

By the time she got home she had a blinding headache.

Going into the house she spoke briefly to Nettie. "I'm going to take something for this headache and lie down."

"Is anything wrong, honey?"

"Oh, Nettie, is anything right?" Turning away to keep her tears private, she went down the hall to the bathroom, swallowed a couple of headache tablets, then continued on to her bedroom where she took off her dress, laid it over a chair and crawled into bed.

Closing her eyes, she prayed for sleep. For blackness and escape. She knew her mood wasn't healthy, but if she didn't escape reality for a few hours she was apt to break down completely, and that wasn't so healthy, either.

Her prayer was answered; she was asleep in minutes.

Once the table in the large dining room was laid with the men's evening meal, including insulated pots of coffee, pitchers of iced tea and water, and dessert, Nettie sat down in the small dining nook to eat her own dinner with Dena. Dena remembered when Nettie ran back and forth from the kitchen to the big dining room, filling coffee cups and water glasses, and serving dessert when it was due. Now she put everything on the table and let the men serve themselves. For a woman her age, and she was no spring chicken, Nettie worked hard. Maybe it was time to do something about that, Dena thought while filling her plate.

"Nettie, would you like some help?"

The older woman looked startled. "Help doing what?"

"I'm talking about an assistant. Someone to set the table and clean up after meals. Someone to do the vacuuming and dusting. That sort of thing."

"Hmm," Nettie said with a frown. "Never gave it any thought."

"But it's a good idea, don't you agree? All you'd have to do is the cooking, which I know you enjoy. You could assign all the tedious work to your assistant."

"I'd still be ordering the groceries and supplies?"

"Yes, of course. Only you know what you need in that department."

"Well, guess I could try it. Mind you, I wouldn't put up with a slugabed. When something needs doing, I want it done right away. And she'd have to be clean. I don't want any dirty fingernails in my kitchen."

"I understand." Dena took a sip of iced tea. "I'll make some calls tomorrow."

They had eaten silently for several minutes, when Nettie said, "You've noticed, haven't you?"

"Noticed what, Nettie?"

"How much I've slowed down. You think I can't do my job anymore."

"Nettie, no! You *should* be slowing down, and you haven't, and that worries me." Dena put down her fork and gave her old friend a heartfelt look. "Nettie, if I lost you, too, I swear I'd just throw in the towel. I know we're not blood related, but you're the only family I have. I want you to start taking it a little easier. In fact, if you decided not to work at all, I'd hire another cook. And you could go on living at the ranch, too. This is your home as much as it's mine."

Nettie reached out and patted Dena's hand. "Thank you, honey, but what would I do all day if I stopped working? An assistant might be a good idea, but I'm not ready to sit in a rocking chair and knit for the rest of my days."

There was another lull, then Nettie said, "That nap must have cleared up your headache."

"It did. I slept for two hours."

"Must have been tired. Didn't you sleep well last night?"

"Not very." Again Dena lowered her fork. "Nettie, so much keeps happening. Every day there's a new shock to deal with."

"Like Tommy dropping in? Who on earth would loan him a car like that?"

"He told me it's his car."

"His! Where would he get money enough to buy an expensive car?"

Dena sighed. "He said his family bought it for him."

Nettie looked utterly amazed. "The Hogan family bought and gave it to him? Good heavens, why?"

"I don't know," Dena said slowly, thoughtfully. "Something else strange occurred today. I ran into Karen Hogan outside the post office, and she seemed so glad to see me there were tears in her eyes. I didn't know what to think. She…"

Nettie threw down her napkin and interrupted Dena with a passionate exclamation. "Those scalawags!"

Dena blinked. "Pardon?"

"Don't you see what they're up to? Dena, you're a smart woman. Put it all together. Who appraised the ranch? Ellen Hogan Clark. Other than your attorney and accountant, who right now is in a better position to know the value of what you inherited? So, almost immediately after the appraisal, along comes Tommy in a shiny new car. Would his driving out here in a rickety old pickup impress you? I'll bet anything he made personal advances. Did he?"

Dena was stunned by Nettie's logic. Why hadn't *she* figured it out? She'd suspected a scheme of some sort, but nothing like this. Apparently it was a final straw to a harrowing day, because she suddenly started laughing, almost hysterically. "They…bought Tommy…a sports car…to impress me," she gasped between gales of laughter. "And Karen…even invited…me…over for dinner."

Nettie began laughing, too. "Those morons," she said. "They put everything they had into a car for Tommy to come a-courtin' in."

"He…asked me out."

"I knew it!"

They nearly collapsed from another spasm of laughter. When they finally calmed down, Dena said while wiping her eyes, "Oh, that felt good. I wondered all day what was going on. I knew something was."

"They've been plotting to get their hands on your inheritance. Through Tommy. Counting on Tommy's charm to woo you back into marriage. Oh, my heavens, imagine if you were gullible enough to be taken in. I'll bet every single one of them would move from town to the ranch."

Dena shuddered. "What a picture *that* makes."

"Horrifying," Nettie agreed. "Well, I haven't laughed like

that in a long time. You're right, it felt good. How did you avoid Karen's dinner invitation?"

"By telling her I was involved with a man who took up all my free time."

"I see." Nettie wore a knowing smile. "You were talking about Ry, of course."

Dena's eyes widened. "How did you come up with that?"

"It's true, isn't it?"

"Um, in a way, yes."

"He was watching you and Tommy today, you know."

"He was?"

"And wearing the darkest scowl I've ever seen on a man's face. Hard to say what was going through his mind."

Dena sucked in a long, uneven breath. "What if he thought the worst?"

"Wouldn't you, if it had been him talking to a pretty, flirty, forward woman?" Noticing Dena's downcast expression, she added, "Hey, chin up there, young woman. It's not over yet. If you want him, fight for him. Ry's a good man, and good men don't grow on trees."

Dena couldn't help laughing again, but there was a weight in her chest that cut her laughter short. If Ry *did* think the worst...oh, what if he did? He wasn't a man to toy with. She knew he had special feelings for her, but she also suspected that he was capable of burying those feelings so deeply they might never resurface.

She had to talk to him, to explain what Tommy's visit had been all about. It would be a miracle if he saw the humor in it, as she and Nettie had, and she was afraid to count on that. He didn't know the Hogans as they did, after all. Oh, there was so much he didn't know, Dena thought with a sudden pang. She should have been more open with Ry all along, even to talking about the rift between Simon and her.

"Would you excuse me for a minute, Nettie?" Rising, Dena laid down her napkin and left the kitchen nook to go to the men's dining room.

Every eye around that table focused on her as she entered.

Her smile included each man, but it was Ry she spoke to. "Please come to the office after dinner. Around eight."

A fearful shiver went up her spine at the frost in his eyes. "Fine," he said stiffly.

She forced herself to smile again. "See you then." To the other men she said, "Sorry for the intrusion."

Back in her chair in the kitchen nook, she said grimly, "I'm going to get this straightened out with Ry or die trying."

Nettie smiled serenely. "Good girl."

Dena sat tensely on the edge of her bed, one hand gripping the spread on each side of her thighs. She had to make Ry understand how little Tommy meant to her. Tommy had come to the ranch uninvited and unexpected. She'd talked to him, yes, but with no more feelings than she would have with a stranger. Ry *had* to believe her. She must *make* him believe her.

How best to accomplish that? she wondered with a frown of uncertainty. An image of her sitting behind the desk and Ry sitting in front of it, and her offering an explanation to his cold and stony face gave her a shiver. Maybe if she started with "I'd like to take that ride you suggested last night," and they got away from the ranch, it would go smoother. Did she care anymore if everyone on the place figured out that their relationship far exceeded normal employer-employee interaction?

"Not a whit," she said under her breath. "Not one damned whit." She got up to pace, at the same time setting up imaginary scenarios for the upcoming meeting. The office, a vehicle or the loft. Which would be best?

She saw her reflection in the mirror above the bureau and stopped in her tracks. After her nap she had put on jeans and an oversize blue T-shirt. Maybe the location of their meeting wasn't nearly as important as how she looked and the method in which she presented that explanation.

Breathless suddenly, she dashed to her closet and began moving hangers back and forth to check out her new clothes. She came to the red dress with the spaghetti straps, form-fitting bodice and full skirt. Her eyes narrowed on it. Dare she be so obvious? She'd bought sexy high-heeled red sandals to wear with it, and wondered afterward if she hadn't lost her mind. She *never* wore clothes like those. Why had she wasted the money?

But all it took to dress like a woman who was proud of her femaleness was nerve. And she had better drum up some courage or she was going to lose Ry.

"No way," she muttered, yanking the dress from the closet by its hanger and laying it out on the bed.

An hour later—it was only a few minutes before eight— she stared at herself in the mirror as though seeing another woman. She had showered, curled her hair, perfumed and lotioned her body, applied makeup that would accent her eyes and the hollows of her cheeks, and then put on the dress and sandals without underwear or hose. Lipstick had been a problem; she hadn't thought to buy a new one when she'd shopped, and her usual pale pink or peach hadn't looked right with the vividness of her outfit. Thus, her lips were as naked as her body under her dress, and she had never felt sexier in her life.

She touched a curl near her ear. Ry had never seen her hair curled like this. Would he like it?

Her glance fell on the clock: 8:02 p.m. Ry would be on time, he always was. With a nervous intake of air, she picked up the knife she'd swiped from the kitchen, strode from her bedroom and down the hall to the office.

The door was open; he was in there waiting for her. She stopped, licked her lips, smoothed her dress, took a big breath and stepped into the doorway.

Ry was sitting in his usual chair, his back to the door. He turned his head, did a double take and then jumped to his feet. There was so much surprise on his face, Dena almost laughed.

"What...?" Ry cleared his throat and began again. "Are you going out?"

"No."

"But you're all dressed up."

"The better to beguile you with, my dear," she said in her best villainess voice. She did it so well, Ry could almost see her twirling a mustache. She had succeeded in rendering him speechless, and he watched mutely while she closed the door and slid the knife under the jamb. They were locked in; no one could open that door unless they used a battering ram.

"Uh...is there a reason for all this melodrama?" Ry asked, trying to sound aloof and not managing it very well.

"Please sit down again," Dena said sweetly.

Perplexed, he sank back onto his chair. She glided over to him and further took the wind out of his sails by bunching up her skirt and straddling his legs. Laying her hands on his shoulders she looked into his stunned eyes and said calmly, "We need to talk."

"Like this?" he croaked. Her scent was filling his head, and her boldness was filling his jeans. He couldn't believe she was capable of such wanton behavior.

"Why not like this?" she said matter-of-factly. "Is my sitting here a distraction? If you don't want me on your lap, just stand up and dump me on the floor."

He glowered into her eyes for a long moment, then making a growling noise in his throat, he clasped her by the waist and pulled her closer. "Now do your talking," he said challengingly.

"I fully intend to." But her voice wasn't the same as before. She made a little sound in her throat in an attempt to clear the huskiness from her vocal cords. "I believe you misinterpreted something that happened today, and I'd like to set you straight."

"You would. Well, go ahead and try. I know what I saw and you can't change that with a few words and some coercive perfume."

She laughed seductively. "No? Let's find out, all right?" She slowly slid her hands from his shoulders to his neck, and then farther up to his face. Dipping her head to place their lips only a breath apart, she whispered, "Tommy wasn't invited to the ranch, nor was I pleased to see him. I asked him to leave, which he eventually did."

"Tommy Hogan? Are you talking about your ex-husband? Is that who that guy was?"

"Oh, dear, I thought you knew who he was." She pressed her mouth to the corner of his lips. "I'm sorry you got the wrong impression and it made you unhappy. I don't want you unhappy, Ry, not about anything. Are you unhappy now?"

A tortured groan rose from his chest. "Dena, this isn't fair. How in hell could I be unhappy with you sitting on top of me?"

Dena chuckled deep in her throat. "Then I'm making you happy. That's very nice to hear. I was so afraid you'd see something in Tommy's visit that wasn't even remotely true."

"You were mighty damned friendly with him."

"Actually, I wasn't. But I don't hate him, Ry. There's nothing to hate. He's still a boy, and—" her hands rose to twine into his hair, tenderly, lovingly "—I've met a man, a real man." What a delight his hair was. Springy and crisply clean, and such a charming mixture of black and silver.

Ry caught the back of her head in his palm, holding it still to search her eyes. "Are you saying...?"

"That I care for you? Yes. That I want you? Yes." She took a breath. "Shall I go on, or should I give you a chance to speak?"

His lips moved, but nothing came out. His heart had started hammering when she'd boldly straddled his legs, but now it felt powerful enough to break through the wall of his chest. She couldn't know what a monumental change had taken place in him since they'd met, nor how his marriage and divorce had adversely influenced his attitude toward women, and how he'd shied from any relationship that even hinted at commitment ever since.

There was an expectancy in her eyes. She wanted to hear how he felt about her. He cleared his throat. "I...got a little crazy when I saw you with Tommy. After last night..." He stopped for a breath. "After last night I guess I thought...I thought—"

"Oh, Ry, say it," she whispered ardently. "Please say it."

He pulled her head forward and kissed her. Her mouth writhed hungrily against his. Desire flamed between them as their tongues met and mated, and she knew, she knew he loved her how ever hard it was for him to say the words.

They were in his mind though. *I love you, Dena. I love you.* And she felt that message in his rough, passionate kisses, and in the possessive way his hands moved over her body, lingering on the smooth skin of her bare shoulders, stroking her back, squeezing between them to caress her breasts through the fabric of her dress. He slid a strap down her shoulder and wet a circular spot with his tongue.

The sensation gave her goose bumps, and her last inhibition flew out the window. She thought about how much she had changed, from an almost prudish, almost old maid to this, a woman who could straddle a man's lap without invitation and then ask him to "Put your hands under my skirt. You'll find a surprise."

"A surprise?" He laughed softly.

"I think you'll like it."

He fumbled around, finally found a section of the hem circling her yards of skirt and slid both hands under it. The pleasure of touching her nude thighs had him closing his eyes, but in the next instant they jerked open.

She smiled into them. "Well?"

"You were right. I like my surprise." While his hands curved around her bare bottom, then teasingly mounted the crease of her thighs and belly to nestle into moist female flesh, open to his touch because of her wanton position on his lap, he nibbled at her mouth. "Damn, you're something," he mumbled thickly. "I came in here tonight all puffed up with resentment and—" he stumbled over the word but finally said it "—jealous."

"Oh, I'm so glad you were jealous," Dena purred.

Her quick comeback was funny and made him laugh. But the seductively purring tone of her voice sank in, and his laughter died a sudden death. She was moving against his hand and seeking his mouth for another kiss. Her own hands wriggled down between them to his belt buckle. Efficiently and expertly, as though she did this every day, she undid his buckle and unzipped his jeans.

They moved this way and that, adjusting their positions for what each knew was coming next. Rosy with passion and breathing hard, Dena pushed down his briefs and freed his manhood. Handling it, stroking it, she quivered. Ry groaned, and to her ears it was a pleasured sound.

"Raise up a little," he instructed hoarsely.

It wasn't a simple accomplishment; her feet were no longer touching the floor. But with his assistance, her hips lifted just enough and he guided his arousal into her. Throwing back her head, Dean moaned and stirred sinuously. Ry yanked down the top of her dress, exposed her breasts and began lavishing them with hot, wet kisses, first one than the other.

"Perfection," he muttered. "Utter perfection." And then he could hold back no longer. "I love you, dammit, I love you."

Her heart nearly exploded with joy. "Damned if I don't love you, too."

They stopped, looked at each other and laughed.

After that nothing much was said for a long, long time.

# Thirteen

---

The next morning Dena saddled a horse and went for a ride. The radiant happiness within her was marred by only one thing, the heartrending fact that her father had died without speaking to her. Oh, he must have forgiven her or he would not have included her in that trust. But if only he could have said so. Of course he hadn't expected death to take him at such a young age. Maybe he'd been planning to call her one day, or to write. She must believe that, she told herself. If she didn't, she would be haunted for the rest of her life.

After an hour or so on horseback, she found herself reining in on the same hill from which she had surveyed the ranch during her first ride after coming home. Leaning forward and patting her horse's neck, she let her gaze drift lazily across the valley. How beautiful it was, the rolling waves of grass, the fields dotted with cattle and horses, the distant mountains in a rainbow of colors, and the compound itself, appearing as toy buildings from this distance. Of course she was going to stay here. That decision, at least, had been made for her. Ry was here, and he loved her as much as she loved him. She considered herself the recipient of a miracle, and sent silent thanks heavenward for Ry Hardin.

And with Ry and the Wind River Ranch, what else could she possibly want?

Sighing because the thing she'd wanted most since leaving home at eighteen was unattainable, she nudged her horse into a walk. She knew she had to stop thinking about it, fretting over something so irrevocable, so fixed in the past. Every yesterday was set in time. She must live for today, and for tomorrow.

Well, the settlement of the estate was in John Chandler's and Terry Endicott's hands. She might hear from Tommy again, or she might not. It didn't matter either way. She was loved by a wonderful man. Things were as good as anyone could hope for, certainly as good as *she* was capable of making them.

Except for one final chore. Dena stiffened at the thought of entering her father's bedroom and clearing away his things, but it was something she had to do, however painful it was going to be. Nettie would do it, but Dena felt driven to do it herself. Maybe it was a form of self-punishment, maybe it was a hope deep within herself that once done she would be able to forget.

It came upon her swiftly and suddenly that she had to get it over with. The longer she procrastinated, the more difficult it would be.

Dena turned her horse toward the compound. Her lips were tight with tension, but she had made up her mind. She would do it today, as soon as she got back.

Ry spotted Dena riding in, and he slipped into the barn and tack room to wait for her to bring in her saddle. He stood behind the door, and when she entered the room a short time later to set the saddle on a rack, he shut the door. She turned with a surprised expression that relaxed into a smile when she saw him.

"Hi," she said breathlessly, feeling him in every cell of her body.

He walked over to her and put his arms around her. "Hi, yourself." His mouth found hers, and their kiss contained so much love, Dena got tears in her eyes.

Ry raised his head to see her. "Are you crying?"

"A little. I love you so much."

"I love you, Dena."

"I know." Every time he said it another empty spot in her body vanished. Small wonder she adored him; he was healing an ailment he didn't even know she possessed.

"And that makes you cry?" he asked in wonderment.

"Am I weird?"

He smiled. "No, you're perfect. Will you come to the loft tonight?"

"Yes," she said huskily. Remembering the reason she'd returned from her ride so soon, she took a backward step. "Do we have any empty cardboard boxes on the place?"

"I'm sure I could scare up a few. What do you want them for?"

Dena looked at the floor. "I—I'm going to clean out Dad's bedroom."

He could tell she was disturbed and unhappy over the job she'd set for herself, and he didn't want her disturbed and unhappy about anything. "Can I help?"

It hadn't occurred to her to ask for Ry's help, but if he was in that bedroom with her, it would all be so much more bearable. A feeling of relief rippled through her, and something else, too, a knowledge so gratifying she again got teary: Through thick and thin, Ry would be there for her, sensing her moods, both good and bad, and offering a shoulder to lean on whenever she needed it, as he'd just done.

"I can't tell you how much I would appreciate your help," she said, sounding choked up.

He immediately went to her and held her, resting his chin on the top of her head. "Don't you know I'd do just about anything for you?"

She snuggled into his warm body, then looked up to peer into his dark blue eyes, so filled with consideration and concern for her well-being. "I'm beginning to."

She felt him take in a big breath of air. His arms tightened around her. Then he said in a near whisper, "Do you think it's a good time for us to talk about getting married?"

Her pulse quickened. She'd known this moment would come, but she'd been thinking of it in terms of *someday*. Marriage wasn't a prerequisite to her happiness with Ry, and she'd overheard his views on the subject, so she never would have pressured him about it. But, oh, it was wonderful to hear him say those words.

"A perfect time," she said with great emotion.

He clasped his hands together in the shallows of her back and looked deeply into her misty eyes. "Will you marry me?"

"Yes."

"Are you going to cry again?"

She shaped a shaky smile. "Maybe."

His sigh was more eloquent than words as he brought her into a closer, more intimate embrace. "I'm happy, Dena."

"So am I," she whispered into his shirt.

He thought of what Nettie had told him of Dena's and Simon's alienation. Dena hadn't mentioned it to him, and he would never breach Nettie's confidence by initiating a conversation about it himself. It was possible that Dena *couldn't* talk about it, not yet, at any rate. He had faith that when she was ready to open that portion of her heart to anyone, it would be with him.

Smiling at her with love and understanding on his face and in his eyes, he took her hand. "Come on. Let's go find those boxes."

Dena steeled herself to open the door to Simon's bedroom. Ry was behind her with a load of cardboard boxes and a package of large, plastic trash bags. The room was dark because of the closed drapes and smelled musty from being shut up. Determined to be mature about this, she went to the windows and drew back the drapes.

Ry set everything in the middle of the room and looked around. Worn carpet covered the floor, and the furniture was heavy, dark wood. There were few decorations—no photographs on the dressers, he noticed right away—an austere room.

"So, where do we start?" he asked.

"Why don't you work on the closet and I'll start on the dressers?" There was a lump in her throat that was difficult to speak around.

"I take it you plan to throw some things away?"

"Dad never did, so I'm sure there are items no one would want."

"Good things in the boxes, then, and the rest in trash bags?"

Dena nodded. She didn't want to see her father's clothing on anyone she knew, so she wasn't sure where the "good" things would end up. Not in this area, though. Maybe she would send them to a charitable organization in Cheyenne. Even the dark, old furniture in this room made her uncomfortable. If she was going to live on the ranch, and she was, she had to make some changes. After the estate was settled and she knew if there was money to spend on new furniture and such, this house was going to get a thorough and complete renovation. So was everything else on the place, especially the loft and tack room.

Ry opened the door of the closet and frowned. "How will I know what's good and what's not?"

"Just use your own judgment." Dena had tentatively approached the high chest of drawers, and her stomach was roiling with nervous tension. Slowly she pulled out the top drawer, and felt relief when she saw that it contained underwear and socks. She went for a trash bag.

Once the chore was started, it wasn't as bad as she'd feared. Ry worked fast, folding wearable jackets, pants and shirts into boxes, and stuffing jeans with holes and shirts that were so faded from age the color was barely discernible into a plastic bag. This job expanded his mind to another. He looked over to Dena, who was kneeling on the floor opening the lowest drawer in the chest. She, too, had been working quickly, it appeared.

"Dena, would you mind if I cleaned out the loft?"

She sent him an adoring smile. "It's already on my list, along with the tack room and any other hidey-holes Dad crammed with junk." The drawer had been slid open, and she suddenly became very still. Ry craned his neck to see what she was looking at.

"What is it, honey?"

"A photo album." Almost tenderly Dena lifted it from the drawer. "It was my mother's." She started turning pages. Ry came over and sat beside her. "These old black-and-whites are pictures of my grandparents and great-grandparents. Oh, there's Mother. She was seven in that picture."

"Are there later pictures of her?" Ry asked.

"There should be." Dena flipped through the pages until she came to one with colored snapshots. She pointed. "That's Mother, shortly before she became ill."

"And that's you next to her?"

"Yes."

"You look like her, Dena."

"Everyone always said so." Her voice turned slightly bitter. "I'm surprised Dad kept any photos of me." She looked at Ry. It was time he knew everything. Her heart beat a little faster, but she forced the words from her mouth. "There's something you don't know. Dad never spoke one word to me since I was eighteen years old."

Ry tried to look dismayed and in the dark about the subject. "Why not?"

"Because I defied him and married Tommy." Dena's eyes glistened with tears. "Oh, Ry, what makes people act the way they do? I never got over Mother dying, and neither did Dad. Instead of mutual grief drawing us together, it tore us apart. The only time we talked was when he had an order to give me or I had some sassy, smart-mouthed remark to throw at him. Life was awful. I couldn't wait to turn eighteen and get away from here."

"You escaped by marrying Tommy," Ry said softly.

"I was a stupid, stupid, stupid girl," Dena exclaimed passionately. "Dad wanted me to go to college. Anything he wanted, I didn't. I think I married Tommy because Dad objected so much to my even dating him." After a pause, she added, "And I've paid for it ever since. The night I walked out of this house to get married, Dad said he would never speak to me again. Who cares, I thought. But I did care, Ry. Once I came to my senses I cared so much it hurt. I wrote and phoned constantly, but it did no good."

Ry put his arm around her and pressed his lips to her cheek. "Honey, you have to put it behind you."

"I know I do, and I'm trying." She swiveled and buried her face in Ry's shirt. He could feel her emotion, her pain, and he wrapped his arms around her. Her words were muffled by his clothing. "He's dead now, and I'll never have the chance to beg his forgiveness."

Ry was silent a moment. "Dena, maybe it was he who should have begged your forgiveness. He was an adult and you were little more than a child. A kid who'd lost her mother and couldn't get over it on her own. Simon should have helped you get through it. Sounds to me like he was mad at the world because his wife died and took his anger out on you. Maybe I'm speaking out of turn, but it's how I feel."

"He was never physically abusive, Ry."

"Sometimes emotional abuse is worse, honey."

"But I was as abusive to him as he was to me."

Ry shook his head. "A sad situation, but he was still the parent and an adult. Your dad was a smart man, Dena, and he should have grasped what was happening before it got so far out of hand."

Dena sighed. "I suppose you're right." She got to her feet and laid the album on top of the dresser. "Let's finish up and get out of here."

Ry uncoiled himself from the floor. "I'm going to take those two filled boxes out to the barn. Unless you want them stored somewhere else."

"The barn is fine. The tack room always stays dry during storms. Maybe you can find room to cram them in there."

"Good enough." Ry stacked the two boxes and picked them up. Loaded down, he maneuvered himself and his burden to the door and left.

The second she was alone, Dena got an eerie feeling. "Don't be a goose," she mumbled, but chiding herself changed nothing. Her mother had died in this room, and while Dena did not believe in ghosts, she couldn't dispel memory. It was too quiet with Ry gone, she decided, and hurried over to the small radio on the nightstand and switched it on.

Music helped, and she turned to the dresser with the mirror. She would let Ry finish clearing out the closet, and she would concentrate on that second dresser, then the nightstand. There really was nothing else, was there? she thought with a crease of sadness between her eyes. Her father, with millions in various banks, had lived very simply. She had run across no personal items of his in any other room of the house. She thought of her apartment in Seattle, and how she had made each small room hers with photographs, books and mementos.

"Oh, well," she said with a poignant sigh, and pulled open a drawer of the mirrored dresser. Her breath suddenly stopped in her throat, for looking up at her was her own face: her graduation picture! Framed in gold and covered in glass. Had she done that before she'd left? She couldn't remember.

And then she began seeing what else the drawer contained: things she'd left behind in her bedroom! She scrambled to take them from the drawer: an orange felt banner imprinted in black with the words Winston High, another that read Go Tigers!, her yearbook, her senior prom dance program, a small box containing costume jewelry that she'd no longer worn, some old sweaters and jeans, a pair of rundown sneakers.

"My Lord," she whispered, stunned beyond sentimentality. Why on earth had Simon kept this old stuff, and in here, his private domain? She was glad to see her senior yearbook, but the rest of it was junk.

There was something else, too, a shoe box. What useless object did *it* contain?

Dena lifted the cover to find out, and nearly fainted. Her letters! She stared into that box for a long time, trying to understand, waiting for her nerves to calm some. She rubbed her hands on the legs of her jeans, for her palms felt sweaty. Finally she gingerly picked up the top envelope and saw that it had been neatly slit open. She wilted. He *had* read her letters!

Had he kept them all? Taking the box from the drawer, Dena sank to the floor. But then something stopped her from immediately delving into it. Nervously, uneasily, she ran her fingers through her hair, unconsciously furrowing it into a facsimile of corn rows. She tried desperately to think, and got stuck on one word: Why? Why, why, why?

Why would he have read her letters and then tucked them away with her old sneakers and prom program? There were so many that the box was full.

She frowned. *The box was full!* She'd written often, but enough times to fill that box? No, she didn't think so. There must be something else in it. She upended the box and the envelopes spilled out into a pile on the floor. That's all there was, envelopes.

But they weren't all addressed to her father. With startled eyes, she picked one up addressed to her. It was in Simon's handwriting, and it was sealed, stamped and ready for mailing.

She put the tips of her fingers to her forehead in a wave of utter agony. He *had* written to her and then never mailed the letter. *Oh, Daddy, why?* After a few moments she got her bearings again and began shuffling through the pile on the floor. There were other envelopes addressed to her, and with her heart in her throat, she transferred them one by one to her left hand. They got to be too many to hold, and she set them on the carpet next to her hip. When she was sure there were no more, she leaned weakly against the dresser and stared at them.

What did this mean? Why would Simon write letters to her and never mail them? Did she want to read them now? What further heartbreak might they contain?

But she had to read them, didn't she? They were the only link she had with her father, and she couldn't destroy them without knowing what he'd put down on paper.

With tears in her eyes she reached for the topmost envelope and slowly slid her thumbnail under the sealed flap. It contained one sheet of paper and was dated over a year ago. It occurred to her then that she would be reading the letters in no particular order. Maybe they had been in chronological order in the box, but she had disarranged any sequence there might have been.

Taking a shaky breath she began reading.

Dear daughter,

I'm a man with destructive pride. Even knowing my own faults so well, I cannot force myself to the telephone when you call, or to call you, or to mail the letters I write in the dark of night, as though daylight would expose my foolish stubbornness to the world.

Dena, your letters are the bright spots of my life. You've done so well for yourself. I know your mother is watching from above with a smile on her beautiful face. I also know that smile is missing when she looks my way. She loved you so much, and if she were still alive, she would be giving me what-for, which I so richly deserve. Of course, if she had lived, none of what took place between us would have occurred. I firmly believe this. You were a sweet child and I was a happy man before her passing. Apparently my beloved Opal was the glue that held our family together.

Every year on my birthday I vow that this is the year I will see you and make amends. I find comfort in visualizing myself going to Seattle and knocking on your door. I know from your letters that you would welcome such a surprise. Dearest daughter, you are very precious to me, and one day I will tell you so.

All my love,
Dad

By the time Dena read the closing she was sobbing. Ry walked in, stopped in shock, then rushed over to kneel on the floor next to her. "What's wrong?" he asked, sounding panicked.

She held out the letter. "Read it." Pulling a tissue from her jeans pocket, she wiped her eyes and blew her nose.

Ry scanned the letter quickly, then fell back on his seat with further shock on his face. "For the love of God," he mumbled.

"There are more." Dena indicated the stack of envelopes beside her. Her eyes teared again. "He did love me, Ry."

Ry felt a bitterness that he couldn't convey to Dena. Why in hell hadn't Simon mailed these letters? "Yes," he said in reply. "It appears he loved you very much."

They looked at each other, then Dena inched closer to him and placed her hands on his chest. "Hold me," she whispered.

He slid his arms around her and felt the internal trembling of her body. Anger erupted within him. Damn Simon Colby for putting her through this! But he realized Dena did not share that anger when she whispered emotionally, "I'm so happy, Ry. No one could know what those letters mean to me."

Ry heaved a sigh. If she was happy over those damned letters, then so was he. But no one was ever going to hurt her again, as her own father had, as long as he, Ryson Hardin, drew breath.

"Dena, let's get married right away."

She pulled back to see his face. "Right away?"

"Yes, let's call my sisters in Texas and have them get together and arrange a simple ceremony for us. We'll fly down. I want you to meet them, in any case, and I'd like them to be at our wedding."

Could anyone be happier than she was at this moment? Was it even possible? "Oh, my love," she said, and nestled closer to his big, warm body. Her soul was at peace for the first time of her adult life. Indeed, there was such a thing as happy endings; she was living one right now.

Ry's lips moved in her hair. "I am your love, and you're mine. Nothing is ever going to change that, Dena. What do you say? Should I call my sisters?"

Dena smiled blissfully. A wedding in Texas. Within a week she would be Mrs. Ry Hardin. "Yes, call them, but kiss me first."

Ry was only too happy to oblige. His mouth covered hers, and her passionate response had his blood boiling in seconds. How he loved this woman, he thought fiercely. Hungrily his hands began roaming her body. She moaned softly as she started slipping deeper into desire.

But then she remembered where they were and broke the kiss. "Tonight," she whispered.

He dropped kisses on her face and felt the moisture of her tears on his lips. His heart ached again for all she'd lived through. She was happy now, and he intended keeping her that way. "I'll call my sisters, then come back in here and help you finish up."

"All right." They scrambled to their feet, but instead of immediately beginning their separate tasks, they found themselves in each other's arms again. This time they stood together, giving to and taking comfort from the other. *He's my rock,* Dena thought dreamily. *My love, my everything.*

And then suddenly she stiffened. "What is it?" Ry asked, as a new wave of alarm shot through his system.

"It's Nettie. Ry, I can't leave Nettie out of our wedding. If we go to Texas..."

It was such a minor glitch in their plans, he couldn't help grinning. "No problem. We'll take her with us."

"Really?" There was a childlike wonder in Dena's voice.

"Honey, I know Nettie's like family to you. Darned right we'll take her with us. Why wouldn't we?"

"But the ranch...the men..."

"The men can fend for themselves for a few days. Or if it would make you feel better, we could hire someone from town to come out and baby-sit them."

Dena looped her arms around his waist and hugged him. "At least cook their meals," she murmured with her cheek against his shirt. "Oh, Ry, you're always going to have the answers, aren't you?"

"I'm always going to be there when you need me," he said. "Count on it."

Dena sighed happily. "I love you so much."

"And I love you." In the next heartbeat she had slipped

away and was heading for the door. "Hey, where're you going?"

She sent him an excited, ebullient smile. "Come with me and find out."

He trailed her into the hall. She was almost running, and he knew then what she had gone to do. Smiling contentedly, he stood there and listened.

"Nettie," she called even before she reached the end of the hall. "Ry and I are getting married in Texas, and you're going with us!"

\* \* \* \* \*

**Bestselling author**

# Joan Johnston

continues her wildly popular miniseries with an
all-new, longer-length novel

### The Virgin Groom

# HAWK'S WAY

One minute, Mac Macready was a living legend in
Texas—every kid's idol, every man's envy, every
woman's fantasy. The next, his fiancée dumped him,
his career was hanging in the balance and his future
was looking mighty uncertain. Then there was the
matter of his scandalous secret, which didn't stand a
chance of staying a secret. So would he succumb to
Jewel Whitelaw's shocking proposal—or take cold
showers for the rest of the long, hot summer…?

Available August 1997
wherever Silhouette books are sold.

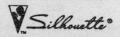

# Take 4 bestselling love stories FREE

## Plus get a FREE surprise gift!

*New York Times* Bestselling Authors

# JENNIFER BLAKE
# JANET DAILEY
# ELIZABETH GAGE

Three *New York Times* bestselling authors bring you three very sensuous, contemporary love stories—all centered around one magical night!

It is a warm, spring night and masquerading as legendary lovers, the elite of New Orleans society have come to celebrate the twenty-fifth anniversary of the Duchaise masquerade ball. But amidst the beauty, music and revelry, some of the world's most legendary lovers are in trouble....

Come midnight at this year's Duchaise ball, passion and scandal will be...

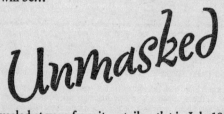

*Unmasked*

Revealed at your favorite retail outlet in July 1997.

# Silhouette makes it easy to heat up those long summer nights!

Clip the attached coupon and receive 50¢ off the purchase of *Hawk's Way: The Virgin Groom* by bestselling author Joan Johnston!

Available August 1997, wherever Silhouette books are sold.

# Coming this July...

# 36 HOURS

## Fast paced, dramatic, compelling...
## and most of all, passionate!

For the residents of Grand Springs, Colorado, the storm-induced blackout was just the beginning. Suddenly the mayor was dead, a bride was missing, a baby needed a home and a handsome stranger needed his memory. And on top of everything, twelve couples were about to find each other and embark on a once-in-a-lifetime love. No wonder they said it was 36 Hours that changed *everything!*

Don't miss the launch of 36 Hours this July with *Lightning Strikes* by bestselling author Mary Lynn Baxter!

Win a framed print of the entire 36 Hours artwork! See details in book.

Available at your favorite retail outlet.

New York Times **bestselling author**

# LINDA LAEL MILLER

Two separate worlds, denied by destiny.

# THERE AND NOW

Elizabeth McCartney returns to her centuries-old family home
in search of refuge—never dreaming escape would lie over a
threshold. She is taken back one hundred years into the past and
into the bedroom of the very handsome Dr. Jonathan Fortner,
who demands an explanation from his T-shirt-clad "guest."

But Elizabeth has no *reasonable* explanation to offer.

Available in July 1997 at your favorite retail outlet.

**MIRA** **The brightest star in women's fiction**

MLLM8

# SILHOUETTE® *Desire®*

# COMING NEXT MONTH

**#1087 NOBODY'S PRINCESS—Jennifer Greene**

Alex Brennan, August's *Man of the Month*, was a white knight looking for a fair maiden to love. Regan Stuart was a beauty who needed someone to awaken her sleeping desires...and Alex was more than willing to rescue this damsel in distress.

**#1088 TEXAS GLORY—Joan Elliott Pickart**

*Family Men*

Posing as sexy Bram Bishop's wife was the closest to marriage headstrong Glory Carson ever wanted to come. But it didn't take much acting to pretend that the most wanted bachelor in Texas was the prince of her dreams.

**#1089 ANYBODY'S DAD— Amy Fetzer**

Mother-to-be Tessa Lightfoot's solo baby parenting plans didn't include Chase Madison, the unsuspecting sperm bank daddy. But if Tessa didn't keep him out of her life, she didn't know how much longer she could keep him out of her bed.

**#1090 A LITTLE TEXAS TWO-STEP—Peggy Moreland**

*Trouble in Texas*

Leighanna Farrow wanted a home, a family and a man who believed in happily-ever-after. Hank Braden wanted Leighanna. Now, the sexiest, most confirmed bachelor in Temptation, Texas, was about to learn what this marriage business was all about....

**#1091 THE HONEYMOON HOUSE—Patty Salier**

For better or worse, Danielle Ford had to share close quarters with her brazenly male colleague, Paul Richards. And his sizzling overtures were driving her to dream of her own honeymoon house.

**#1092 UNEXPECTED FATHER—Kelly Jamison**

Jordan McClennon was used to getting what he wanted, and he wanted former flame Hannah Brewster and the little boy he thought was his son. But when the truth came out, would it change how he felt about this ready-made family?